Scarlet Wind

Scarlet Wind

Frances Burke

ROBERT HALE · LONDON

© Frances Burke 2009
First published in Great Britain 2009

ISBN 978-0-7090-8805-9

Robert Hale Limited
Clerkenwell House
Clerkenwell Green
London EC1R 0HT

www.halebooks.com

The right of Frances Burke
to be identified as author of this work has been
asserted by her in accordance with the
Copyright, Designs and Patents Act 1988

2 4 6 8 10 9 7 5 3 1

Typeset in 11/15½pt Palatino
Printed in Great Britain by the MPG Books Group, Bodmin and King's Lynn

PREFACE

A WET WIND howled through the trees in the Great Park, loosening tiles from the roof of the chateau and cooling the stone paving baked by a summer sun. My footsteps raced along with the wind, through the open gates and up the long gravelled drive to the entrance. Here I pounded to make myself heard above the voice of the storm and, once admitted, flew up the grand staircase on feet that barely touched the marble slabs. The great rooms were silent and bare. No one followed as I climbed ever higher to the north tower, fearful of what I'd find.

Panting, clutching the stabbing pain under my ribs, I flung open the double panelled doors and raced into the circular chamber. Several dozen flames in great stands of candelabra flickered wildly, and a serving woman hastened to slam the doors shut. I hardly noticed. All my attention was on the woman lying on the bed.

The air was thick with heat and the sound of laboured breathing that quickened into a moan, then to a rising arpeggio of shrieks that tore at the nerves like the rasping of violin strings in the hands of a maniac. Two other women standing helplessly at the bedside covered their ears beneath their caps, watching their mistress writhing amongst the tangled bedsheets, waiting for the monstrous sounds to die away.

Her cries ceased suddenly and she collapsed back against the pillows in exhaustion.

I ran to her, dropping my shoulder pouch at the bedside and leaning close to look into that fondly remembered face, but I barely recognized my childhood friend.

'Camille! Why did you wait to send for me? My poor girl, what have they done to you?' I smoothed her wet hair and hid my dismay. Certainly it had been seven years, but the rounded cheeks and sweetly bowed mouth I recalled were now thinned and grey with strain, and the ringlets I'd so envied were as limp as straw left to moulder in the field.

Blue eyes dulled by pain looked up. Camille tried to smile but the effort seemed almost too great. 'Juliette,' she whispered. 'You came.'

'Of course! I'd have come earlier had I known you were here. Why have you returned to your old home for your lying in? Where is your husband?' Without waiting for a reply I turned on the two women servants, their neat striped gowns and crisp fichus an insult to the condition of the woman they supposedly attended. 'Why do you stand about idly? What have you done for milady?'

The younger maid, looking frightened, tried to hide behind her companion, who adopted a truculent attitude. 'We've done everything a body might, but the babe doesn't come. We've tried burnt feathers, and pepper to make Madame la Comtesse sneeze—'

Untying my cloak, I rummaged in the leather pouch, saying impatiently, 'How far advanced is the birth? Where is the midwife?'

The serving woman shook her head, allowing a few grey locks to escape her cap. 'There be nobody but us. Madame la Comtesse arrived here at noon yesterday and was brought to bed in that very hour. But as you see, the house is shut up and everyone gone. By God's grace we'd stayed to ... to see that all was tidy.'

'She's been labouring for nigh on thirty-six hours, without help?'

At the fury in my tone, the woman stepped back. Her voice turned to a whine. ''Tis not my work. I brought candles and meat and drink.' She pointed to an untouched tray at the bedside.

I swallowed my rage. These women were ignorant kitchen maids, or some such, unaccustomed to thinking beyond their immediate surroundings. They probably believed they had done their best. Turning back to Camille, I drew down the sweaty coverlet and raised the hem of her nightgown, saying softly, 'I must examine you, dear, if I'm to help you.'

Camille grasped at my wrists. 'Wait! 'Tis coming again. Oh, dear Lord in Heaven, 'tis upon me.' Her voice rose to a wail and kept on rising.

I waited, feeling the fingers tighten on my wrists, but with a pitiful lack of strength. Camille was clearly almost done. Even her screams lacked their previous edge. When the paroxysm had passed, I made my examination. My hands greased with goose fat, I spread Camille's legs and felt my way into the birth canal to touch the head of the child. It was wedged tightly. As the ripples of the next contraction began I knew that the child could not move. If something were not done, Camille and her baby would die together very soon.

The responsibility was mine. There was no one else.

Withdrawing my hand, I reached for the pouch, saying over my shoulder, 'Bring two stands of candles close and snuff the others. And open a window. The room is a furnace.'

The women obeyed, the older one peering curiously at the slack figure of Camille. 'She's dying, eh? And the babe with her?' Her callousness was that of the peasant living close to nature and its cruelties. Still, it grated.

'She will not die! Bring me hot water and clean linen, and make haste.'

'But the fire is out.'

'Then rekindle it.'

Grudgingly, the women departed, leaving me with my patient.

My patient, I thought. How strange that the first time responsibility for a life had devolved on me alone it should be Camille de Cassonnière, dear childhood friend who stood in desperate need. If only Father were here. But he was dead and gone and his training and craft were in my hands, his legacy to the world held by a mere woman. I looked down at those hands, steady, capable. I was equal to this. I had to be.

Kneeling at the bedside, I turned Camille's sunken face towards me.

'I can help you, dear Camille. Trust me. Now look at the silver pin at my throat. Do you see it flash as I move? Watch the pin. Follow its movement.' Fighting back my concern, I let my voice fall into a soothing cadence as I slowly turned my head from side to side, causing the pin to glint in the candlelight. With Camille's eyes tracking its path, I continued to speak soothingly, drawing a picture of contentment, of wandering down a garden pathway towards a distant goal, watching as my friend's eyelids drooped and she accepted the suggestion that she was now drifting in a landscape where there was no ugliness, no pain, only complete and utter rest.

Her breathing had slowed even as the next contraction began. When a frown gathered and she began to stiffen, I continued the quiet, even flow of words, carrying Camille beyond present travail to a place of calm. Seeing her eventually completely relaxed, I rose and removed the wrapping from a peculiar-looking metal grip that had lain in my pouch. With a brief prayer to the God whose existence I doubted, I slipped the

8

horseshoe-shaped instrument into the birth canal, feeling my way carefully. When I came to the child's head I manoeuvred the forceps until the leather-padded teeth closed about the skull, then began to pull.

Nothing happened. I made a slight adjustment, and pulled again. Slowly, very slowly, I exerted more pressure. The strain on my arms was huge, as was the stress in my mind. I'd never done this before. Theory was all very well, but the instrument had only recently come into my father's hands, through the payment of a huge bribe to the family of physicians who had devised the procedure. He'd had no opportunity to try it before the apoplexy had struck him down.

Sweat dripped into my eyes. I shook my head to clear the droplets – and felt the wedged child give! Slowly, carefully I continued to exert pressure until, with a sudden gush of bloody fluid, the head and shoulders appeared. Minutes later I held Camille's little son as he gave his first cry.

When the door of the chamber opened for the maids, Camille was lying gazing down at the new arrival while I busied myself with the aftermath of the struggle.

The two servants stood open-mouthed, almost dropping their burdens. I turned to them, saying matter-of-factly, 'As you see, Madame la Comtesse has been safely delivered of a son. You may help me to wash her and change the linen.' I couldn't keep the relief from my voice. I'd done it! I'd saved a mother and child who would have died if I'd not been there. Father's training was vindicated. And now my vocation was clear. Whatever the world might think, a woman could be a doctor of medicine. Somehow, I wasn't yet sure how, I would find a way to follow the profession, bringing hope to the suffering.

I looked down at Camille's absorbed expression as I drank in the glory of the child nestling in her arms, and felt infinitely rewarded.

CHAPTER 1

I ENTERED PARIS on horseback via the Porte Royale on a cool and cloudy September morning, excited to be there at last, yet feeling some trepidation. The area around the gates was crowded with market carts bringing in produce, although a meagre enough array, and I had to push my way through.

I smiled to see washerwomen and girls on errands with their skirts kilted above their sabots flirting with soldiers of the National Guard. Things were no different between the sexes than in my own village. My ears rang with the unaccustomed noise of vendors and vehicles, and the overpowering smells from the gutter made my eyes water. Still, people seemed happy, if ragged, and there was a sense of freedom in the air. Stories of breadlines and unrest had filtered out to the countryside to colour my expectations, but now I relaxed in the saddle and enjoyed the market day atmosphere.

My male dress, courtesy of my older brother's discarded wardrobe, fitted well, and I felt comfortable in my new role of Doctor Jules Roussel as I picked my path through the crowd. I'd been on the road for some days and had finally reached my goal, the capital, heart of the great Revolution bringing equality and brotherhood to the nation.

It would happen, I had no doubt, although already there were rumours of power struggles amongst the newly elected members of the National Convention. Of course, one must expect some ambitious jostling for position. It was all so new, this government of the people by the people. With centuries of monarchy wiped out, there was bound be some trial and error before the infant Republic could stand securely on its feet. The pity was that King Louis and his family must be incarcerated, being considered untrustworthy since their attempted flight fourteen months ago. I wasn't quite comfortable with this, but reassured myself that once political order was established the king would eventually be allowed to retire in peace.

Fifty metres further on I reined in and surveyed the unprepossessing cobbled street and grimy buildings leaning in upon one another to block the sunlight. As a gateway to a great city it was hardly an inspiring sight. Yet the distant skyline wore a frieze of important buildings, church spires and elegant hotels, once the metropolitan dwellings of the privileged and now turned over to public use. I drew in a breath of anticipation and urged the horse on.

I was unsure of my destination. I just knew there would be a place for me to set up a practice and begin the work for which Father had fitted me. My confidence had been boosted by my achievement in saving little Jean-Claude de Cassonnière and his mother. Of course, I had no illusions about the need for subterfuge if I wanted to be accepted in the male profession of medicine. The villagers would have hounded me out if I'd set up amongst the people who knew me as a woman. The obvious solution was to go where there was great need and where I was unknown. Hence my arrival in Paris on this balmy morning, my unruly chestnut hair rolled above my ears then tied to fall neatly down my back, and wearing the hat, coat and breeches of a young man of middle class up from the country to view the metropolis.

I was an experienced rider, since my father had required my

company when visiting the sick, and he'd no patience with side-saddles, which he considered insecure. So I'd been an accustomed sight riding astride, pantaloons modestly hidden by skirts – just another eccentricity of Dr Roussel. Of course, riding like a man was one thing. Carrying off the whole imposture was a matter for deep thought and continual awareness. Still, so far there'd been no problem. I thrust down my insecurity and concentrated on finding a passage through the raucous crowd.

It was difficult to make my way without my horse knocking people aside and trampling them. Carts and tumbrels fought for room, those piled with the waste and ordure of the city clearing a path by the nature of their loads. Some carriages forced a passage, with drivers shouting their warning to stand aside, and being roundly cursed. But the greater part of the crowd was on foot, wood sellers bent over with their wares strapped to their backs, water vendors and hawkers of all kinds, women with baskets of washing on their heads, bakers' boys balancing their goods high above thieving hands, shrilling catcalls at one another. My horse and I were jostled and I was beginning to feel overwhelmed.

Catching sight of a roof that promised a palatial building, and therefore some public space surrounding it, I did some pushing of my own away from the relatively wide Rue St Jacques to wind through dark, narrow, less crowded streets.

As I penetrated deeper into the maze, I started to feel uneasy. I could so easily become lost in this crooked warren. I wasn't even sure whether I'd turned back on myself. Perhaps I should have stayed on a street that at least headed in the right direction. The noise of the crowds would have been reassuring. Here, there was no one about, and only the clatter of my horse's hoofs on the cobbles to disturb the dank air of the alleys. I felt a chill between my shoulder blades that had nothing to do with the weather.

Then, without warning I emerged into a small square where a set of gates led to a magnificent formal garden overlooked by a palace. Cheered, I followed the wall down to the end, only to find myself in another labyrinth of alleys and by-ways. Now I really was lost. My unease transferred to my mount, which sidled and jibbed at the bridle. I patted his neck and told myself to stay where I was and take stock. Surely the river was *that* way.

An outbreak of noise in the distance made me start. Voices shouting, and a lot of crashing. It sounded like a riot. I saw an old man sitting in a nearby doorway smoking his pipe, and leaned down to him. 'Tell me, monsieur, does the river lie straight ahead? And can I get there from this street?'

He removed his pipe, hawked and spat, then revealed the stumps of two teeth in a grin. 'Just follow your nag's head, lad, and you're like to see some fun along the way.'

'Thank you. But what do you mean?'

With a shrug, the man clamped the pipe back between his gums and closed his eyes.

I moved on quickly. The riotous sounds had increased, pierced with shrieks. The chill between my shoulder blades had turned to a piercing arrow of ice. What was going on? And where were the people who would normally be going about their business, or just leaning from the windows gossiping?

As the volume of noise rose, my horse threw up its head, ready to wrest itself from my control. I fought the animal with trembling hands. Surely those were screams of fear and torment! Forcing my mount around a corner into another, wider street, I looked down to see the gutter running scarlet. The metallic smell hit me. Blood! The gutter ran with enough blood for a slaughterhouse! What in the name of all the saints was happening?

A running figure appeared out of an alley and cannoned into the horse, clutching wildly at my stirrup as the animal reared, almost unseating me. Fighting to maintain my balance, I looked down into the face of a scrawny child, white with terror.

I said, sharply, 'What is it? What has happened?'

The child couldn't speak. Mouthing soundlessly, he tried to climb up my boot, his grimy little hands and feet scrabbling for purchase. I looked up the street and saw his pursuers, a group of men as wild-eyed as pirates and armed with bloodied knives and staves. Reaching down, I grasped the child by his ragged shirt and hauled him up behind me, digging in spurs and heading down the slippery cobbled slope. The horse skidded and recovered, carrying us rapidly away from the band of killers.

I was breathless by the time we arrived at the bridge across the Seine. Oblivious to the sight of magnificent buildings and the great cathedral towering over the Ile de la Cité, I reined in. Having made sure we were not followed, with some difficulty I succeeded in detaching the child clinging to my back. I then dismounted to survey my tattered prize.

Big scared eyes looked back at me.

I said, as reassuringly as I could from a dried throat, 'I want to help you. Tell me what was going on back there. Why were those men chasing you?'

The boy, who could hardly have been more than nine years old, licked his lips and muttered, 'They just broke in and started killing … they never said why … they just started in to bash us.' His voice broke on a sob and he covered his eyes with one skinny arm.

'Broke in where?' My tone was gentle, hiding a horror that crept over me like a wave of insects, raising the hairs on my body.

'The prison, l'Abbaye.' He gulped. 'They cut off Grand-père's head and it rolled on the ground—'

I choked. *Mère de Dieu*! What kind of place had I come to, that such things could happen? Swallowing my outrage, I said, 'I'm so sorry.' So inadequate. But what else was there to say? I waited a moment, and added, 'Do you have a home to go to? Is there someone there for you?'

The boy looked up imploringly. ''Tis a long way, right across the town.'

The poor lad wanted a ride. Well, so be it. Remounting, I beckoned him to come up behind me. 'You must show me the way. I'm a stranger to Paris, you know.'

The sun was high by the time I'd been directed across the city through elegant thoroughfares arcaded with glittering shop-fronts, on to smelly market halls, and more twisting alleys beyond, to the insalubrious quarter of Saint-Antoine.

The boy stayed silent for most of the time. However, when I began to question him, as kindly as possible, he did answer. It seemed he was known as 'Jaseur', although, for the moment, little Chatterbox had had all talkativeness scared out of him. I did learn that his brother had gone to fight the war against the Prussians, leaving him as sole support to a sick mother and frail grandfather. So it didn't take much guesswork to see why he, a child without the capacity to earn more than a few sous running errands, would end up in prison.

'Did you steal food, Jaseur?' I asked.

He hung his head.

'And Grand-père?'

He looked up and nodded. It appeared the old man had been caught doing some more sophisticated thieving. Now the boy was worried about his mother, alone and unable to work.

Before I could sort my feelings about this situation, we arrived at the house of Mme Poisson, who enveloped Jaseur in an enormous hug, before throwing herself upon my neck and weeping her joyful gratitude. She was a big woman, with the roundness of a cottage loaf and creases of good humour in her face, now that anxiety had been relieved. Her ill health showed in her hobbling gait and wheezing breath, but she was hospitable. Once both she and Jaseur had recovered, she insisted his rescuer should enjoy the almost undrinkable coffee she brewed to accompany a single stale bun, which was eaten out of politeness.

When the tale had been told, Grand-père grieved for with a brevity that spoke volumes, and I had fended off another embrace, I was able to mention my own affairs. I'd seen that, despite poor health, the widow kept a clean house. Before long, Doctor Jules Roussel had broached the idea of renting two rooms and setting up a surgery in just the sort of district I'd envisaged – heavily populated, poor and disadvantaged. The Saint-Antoine suburb was extremely crowded; the horse would have to go. However, I was accustomed to walking long distances. My needs were few, and I had money enough to support me until I was established.

And truth to tell, I needed space to recover from my own shock. Was it only an hour since I rode through the city gate so expectantly? I felt as if I'd aged a year since then and must struggle to regain some of my faith in humanity.

The widow, however, looked relieved and delighted at her good fortune, and heaved herself up a rickety stair to display the third-floor rooms. The doors might be rat-eaten and the sagging roof beams a danger, but there was no dust to be seen. Each chamber had one small, square window giving on to the cobbles below, and there was even a fireplace, clearly unused for a long time. Furnishings were basic: cot, chest and a wobbly chair squeezed into one room, nothing in the other. I suspected that I would be moving into the late Grand-père's quarters.

The tiny, empty room, perhaps belonging to the soldier son, argued a sale of contents to provide food and necessities. The

starkness told the tale of poverty. I wondered how many families in the district carried on the same struggle for survival, and
felt again the burning anger I'd known all my life at the inequal-
ities created by mere circumstances of birth.

It was then I decided to take cosy Mme Poisson into my confidence. I had to trust someone, and she was likeable and, of
course, stood in debt to me. So I laid out my plan for a double
life. I could not entirely abandon my femininity, and I needed to
be able to slip from my role upon occasion. One room would
house Doctor Jules Roussel and his medical equipment. The
other would be the domain of his sister, Juliette, a young
woman who worked as a seamstress.

My new landlady could not have been more helpful. Clearly,
she hid romantic leanings beneath her vast bosom, as well as a
maternal instinct that I'd need to watch if I didn't want to be
smothered.

She patted my sleeve. '*Hé* but you make a pretty boy, *mon
chou*. In your skirts you must be a veritable beauty.'

This was going too far. My skin was smooth and fair and I
owed my hair and a pair of wide brown eyes to my mother. Yet
I'd been told my mouth was far too wide and adapted to stub-
bornness, courtesy of Father; and my height and slender build,
although an advantage for my masquerade, were not in the
accepted mould of dainty, yet opulent Venus. However, I
accepted the compliment meant so kindly.

As for Jaseur knowing about my double life, the little imp
was, I guessed, the repository of more neighbourhood secrets
than an egg is full of meat. This was just another bit of knowledge added. Besides, man or woman, I'd rescued him from
certain, brutal death. I didn't need to see him cut his finger and
cross his thin breastbone with his blood to know that my secret
was safe with him.

Downstairs again, Mme Poisson paused at the door to say, 'A

word of warning, dear *docteur*. The old ways are gone and now we are all *citoyen* and *citoyenne*.'

I nodded. I'd known the old forms of address were forbidden, but found it difficult to remember, especially in the little backwater village I'd come from, where change was generational. 'I shall remember, *Citoyenne*.'

The woman smiled. 'To my friends I'm known as Mère Poisson.'

The next five days and nights would be scoured into my memory, much as I'd like to have blotted them out. They became known as the 'September Massacres', and the horror of them struck the minds of ordinary citizens who had not been part of the cut-throat gangs sweeping through the city's prisons on a murderous spree that accounted for some 1500 men, women and children.

There was no reason for it beyond the senseless, mindless brutality of a mob fired up with tales of treachery against our country; and the monstrous tide of killings changed my thinking. According to rumour, most of the victims had been common folk either imprisoned for minor offences, or deliberately rounded up off the streets as suitable fodder. If such things could be ordered by the men who controlled the municipal government of Paris, the Commune, then the great plan for the Republic was dangerously flawed.

However, I was new to the political hub of the country. Rumour was not proof, and there could be an explanation. Maybe. Although sickened, for the moment I put aside doubts. My main objective must be to set up my practice and begin earning a living.

My first patient was my landlady, whose breathlessness clearly indicated enlargement of the heart from dropsy. The regular administration of a tincture of digitalin, obtained from the nearest apothecary, who seemed bemused by this use of a

herb normally used in an ointment for scabby head, brought
great relief. It led to my praises being sung around the neighbourhood, and brought an influx of sufferers seeking treatment.
Forever trying new ways to combat sickness and pain, I soon
built a reputation. However, my already weakened trust in the
great revolutionary plan was dealt a terrible blow one evening
by my youngest admirer, Jaseur.

He poked his tousled head into my room, saying urgently,
'Citoyen Docteur, there's someone to see you.'

I sighed. It had been a long day and I'd just shut the door on
the last of a series of quinsy sufferers, their swollen throats and
pain-filled eyes a reproach when I had no cure for them. It
usually attacked the young, whose hold on life was frail
enough, without adequate food and shelter. These were often
the non-paying patients, the street children, who tugged at my
heart and made me long for a magic potion to cure all their
many ills.

Stretching and easing my back, I said, 'Bring him or her in,
Jaseur—'

'No. You don't understand. He can't stay. He says there's a
message for you, from your brother.'

'From Philippe!' Was I glad, or merely surprised? I couldn't
tell. It had been so long since he'd left home for the seminary,
not even returning when Father died. I doubted whether we
should recognize one another. 'Where is this messenger?'

'In the alley. He says he can't wait. They're after him.'

'Who? Never mind. I'm coming.'

Rushing outside into the dark, I almost toppled the cowled
figure crouched against the alley wall as if trying to melt into
the filthy stones.

'Who are you? How did find me?'

A whispering voice answered, ''Twas not difficult. I know
who you are, "Docteur" Roussel. I was with your brother when

those animals broke into the Carmes prison, and I was the only one to escape over the wall. I have been in hiding ever since, here in Faubourg Saint-Antoine, where you are becoming quite well known.'

I felt a frisson right up my backbone. 'You are a brother priest? You say Philippe is dead?'

The cowled figure nodded. 'I leave Paris tonight. Yet I could not go without telling you that his last thoughts were of you.'

'That was kind.' I couldn't go on. I was surprised at the flooding surge of grief for the older brother I'd scarcely known.

'Father Roussel spoke often of his young … sibling. The one trained by his father in medical skills.'

I stiffened. Would he give me away? Was that why he had come?

'He did not know you were in Paris. But I have since heard of your work amongst the poor and I knew you must be the one.' The priest's whispering voice faded. 'I wish you well in your profession, Docteur Roussel. Do not doubt your brother is with God. *Adieu.*' He melted into the shadows.

So he knew, I thought, and he would not betray me. He was a rare and generous man as well as a man of God. But oh, the grief for Philippe, who had died in such a horrible way. Now there was no one left, only me with my father's legacy, which must be put to good use.

And now I knew just how I would do it.

CHAPTER 2

SIX WEEKS LATER I'd settled into my new position as medical inspector of one of Paris's most notorious prisons, the Conciergerie. Set right in the heart of the city on the Ile de la Cité, this medieval fortress, part of the Palais de Justice, had housed criminals for several hundred years. Now it was known as the Antechamber to Hell and, as far as I knew, no one who had entered it had ever escaped. Most of its inmates were of the nobility, destined to spend their last days in the cells and common areas beneath the Great Hall, where the Revolutionary Tribunal daily drew up its lists of those who would be tried, sentenced and executed, all within twenty-four hours.

I had not wanted to tend these prisoners of the privileged class. I'd grown up in the shadow of my friend Camille's father, the owner of lands and people for leagues around his country estate. A heartless abuser of his power, he was much hated. My own loathing of inequality was rooted in a child's observation of his mistreatment of others. But he was not blind to the temper of the people. Foreseeing his own future should the Revolution take hold, he fled the country without warning and with much of his wealth, which explained why Camille had found her old home abandoned when she'd returned to seek support.

Added to that, her husband, newly elected as delegate to the National Assembly in Paris, had not hesitated to leave his wife behind as she was on the point of giving birth. It was so typical of the carelessness and egocentricity of the ruling class, I believed. The aristos were a stain on the nation, and I had little sympathy for them.

However, despite my wish to serve in the prisons of the common folk, where conditions were dreadful and many died before coming to trial, I was given no choice. The Revolutionary government wanted its prime victims in good health when they went to public execution. They were not to cheat Madame Guillotine of her prey. And Citoyen Docteur Roussel was to see to it.

Each day as I entered the great arched and groined halls of the Conciergerie I had to suppress a shiver. The atmosphere and surroundings depressed me. I could fancy the cold stones having absorbed the misery of countless unfortunates down through the centuries. Their ghostly agonized cries and groans sounded in my ears with an awful reality. Imprinted on my mind were images of the rack and the fires heating cruel instruments of torture, and I could not shake them off.

I hated the Conciergerie and the men who went about the business of condemning their fellows to decapitation and loss of identity in a mass grave, without even the remotest hint that they cared. The torture of the inhabitants was no less real for being mental, rather than physical. I always hurried through the hallway, which was the principal axis of the prison, and beyond to the separate yards. At least I need not concern myself over my imposture. No one had the slightest interest in me, once my credentials were established. I was a factotum, a servant of the State, and therefore practically invisible.

Once in the prisoners' courts, I felt as though time had slipped back and I was caught up in a social event as, dressed in the rags of their finery, the prisoners promenaded and engaged in elegant conversation. Witty discussion vied with gossip and flirtation in the corner where members of both sexes could meet and converse through the gates. During the day, card games were a common pastime, as well as musical or play-acting groups. I could not help but admire their sangfroid in the face of impending death.

Today, conscious as ever of being watched by the guards, I did not bow to the approaching woman whose coiffure and lace at her elbows and bosom proclaimed her gentility. Instead, I greeted her with a cool, 'Bonjour, citoyenne. Did your daughter pass a more comfortable night?'

The former marquise, her once famed cheekbones now sharp, but still retaining a certain haggard beauty, inclined her head. Her haughty manner couldn't conceal her anxiety. 'She suffers so much, my poor Louise. Will you come to her, m'sieur?'

I nodded briefly, keeping to the formality which I used to distance myself. Not only was I wary of an inadvertent discovery of my masquerade, but I guarded myself against my emotions. I still could not watch the suffering of children without inward pain.

We passed through the crowded court where fashionable ladies strolled as if taking the air at Versailles. There a fountain played, and children were absorbed in games, or listening to an older girl reading to them from a precious volume saved from the inferno, for some had quite literally had their homes burned down around them, and been dragged off to prison with nothing more than the clothes they wore. Two or three ladies had spread wet garments to dry on the stone tables near the fountain, apparently unfazed by the necessity of doing their own washing. Others simply sat and stared into space, their thoughts clearly far from their present surroundings.

I followed my companion into one of the cells overlooking the courtyard, knowing what I would see. A girl of about twelve tossed feverishly on her straw pallet, eyes bandaged, her sweat-soaked hair matted around a face marred by a heavy red rash. Heedless and unaware, she drifted in another time frame, whispering to herself.

Kneeling, I turned back the cover, raising the girl's hands to expose the palms. 'The rash has spread,' I said. 'It's the typhus fever.'

The mother bent to smooth the wet hair. 'Can you do nothing for her? She feels such pain in her head, and the light is an agony to her. I keep her blindfolded during the day and sponge her and try to have her drink—'

I covered the girl and rose, noting with approval the cell's cleanliness. Stark as the stones were, they were well scrubbed, and there was no odour from straw or bedding. Nevertheless, a reminder would not hurt. I said, '*Citoyenne*, as you have seen, this fever is common in prisons and, indeed, any other place where numbers of people must live in close contact. I believe that the answer lies in keeping to the strictest hygiene. 'Tis essential that your clothing and your person should be kept as clean as possible.' There was no need to mention the constant battle with lice.

The marquise stiffened. 'I have done as you advised, and so have many of my friends. The head jailer has issued orders for the cells to be washed down regularly with vinegar, and we take care of our garments ourselves. The palliasses are aired daily.'

'And your hair, *citoyenne*?' I was brusque. I knew I was giving offence, yet the matter was too important for such a concern. It was my job to stop the dreaded jail fever from sweeping through the prison and depriving the state Executioner of his work. It was an ignoble use of my calling, but it did give me the opportunity to develop an idea stirring in my mind.

The marquise stared down her nose at me. 'We brush our hair thoroughly each day and rinse it without using soap, as you advise.'

I nodded in acknowledgement. The powder and lacquers normally used for the elaborate and insanitary court hairstyles were scarcely available here, which was just as well. Great ladies had been known to keep their coiffures undisturbed long enough for all manner of creatures to take up residence, from roaches to mice. And as for the wigs! They might have been alive.

I said, 'Then you are doing all in your power to remain healthy. There have been other cases of the fever, although my orders to the jailers have helped to forestall a true epidemic. I congratulate you upon your good sense, *citoyenne*.'

The worried mother had overcome the haughty aristocrat. 'My daughter … she is no better. I beg of you, *m'sieur—*'

My smile cut off the woman's pleading. 'She will recover. This fever is seldom fatal to children.'

'*Le bon Dieu* be thanked! You are sure?'

Inwardly I rejoiced, although I was careful to maintain my professional image. 'If you keep to the regimen I have suggested, and continue to care for her as you have done, I can be sure. The fever will run its course, perhaps for another ten days, and she will be weak, but if you send out for good nourishing broth and milk, her strength will return.'

The woman turned away to hide the emotion revealed in her voice as she murmured, 'To what avail? She will only live to take her place in the tumbrel with other innocents and be borne away to her death.'

'As to that—' I was interrupted by a wavering voice from the bed.

'*Maman*! Where are you, *Maman*?'

'Here I am beside you, *chérie*.' The marquise flew to her daughter, and I took a step backward. Moved by the woman's distress, I'd almost made a mistake. It was too soon to speak. This idea of mine … it was crazy, and yet it stayed with me, nagging, demanding to be considered. I took from my bag a soothing decoction of honey and elderflower and, placing it at the bedside, quietly left the cell. There were other calls to be made, other people to be helped.

Outside, the autumn sun had barely crept above the roofline of the buildings enclosing the courtyard. Five storeys high, they cast a shadow for most of the day, and the arched colonnade around three sides created a chill and gloomy passageway. I shivered. Winter was coming, but not for these inhabitants. I stopped to watch the children playing catch ball and felt a knife-like pain in my heart. What had these innocents done that their lives should be brutally cut off amidst a jeering crowd?

My lack of sympathy for their elders warred with my need to save life and I felt horribly divided. Moreover, lately I'd come to envisage the Revolution as some kind of bloated monster in its pursuit of revenge. Was it not unjust for any one sector of the community to mow down another? Where was the promised brotherhood? Where was the balance in a regime that stripped everything, including life, from fellow Frenchmen, and placed power in the hands of the few? Where was the gain?

I thought sorrowfully of my brother, Philippe, a gentle man who had loved God and wanted to bring Him into the lives of others. How much poorer the world was for the loss of people like him. And it wasn't only the nobility and the priesthood who suffered. Citizens whose only crime was to speak out against injustice, or even merely to have had some association with aristocratic clients, were housed in the many prisons of Paris awaiting trial and execution. There were constant tales of neighbour informing on neighbour, of apprentices, guild masters, lawyers, beggars, prostitutes, honest burghers and their families swept up without warning. My faith in the great Revolution was being undermined daily as I went about my work, both in the prison and in the streets.

With a sigh, I continued my rounds, visiting women sick with repressed terror for themselves or loved ones, others whose worsening cough and wizened appearance presaged an early end to their death watch. I anointed childish cuts and abrasions and sparred verbally with an elderly dowager whose crippled limbs didn't affect her wits or her enjoyment of a wicked tale or two exchanged with a personable young man. The bravery in those faded old eyes hurt me as much as the laughter of the children. This day I was glad to leave the women's yard and move on to the men.

On my first visit there I'd been nervous and very conscious of the need to preserve my male identity, extending my stride and addressing the guards with authority. However, I need not have worried about the prisoners, many of whom were of the aristocracy. As the lords of creation, they barely acknowledged my presence. If forced to do so, through illness, they treated me as an employee and were not noticeably grateful for my help.

Forced to hide my annoyance, I recalled my father's dictum that gratitude was merely a bonus; and fortunately, I had my other patients of the streets and alleys of the poorer faubourgs to remind me where my true work lay.

Today I was greeted by another crippled ancient with a demand for something to be done about his gout.

Waving his stick at me, he hobbled forward, face reddened and wig askew. 'The potion you gave me is useless! Useless, do you hear? You are a charlatan, *m'sieur*. I'd dismiss you instantly were it in my power to replace your incompetent person.'

I hid a smile. Life with Father had taught me to handle eccentric older men.

'*Mille pardons, citoyen*. I will try another method. Shall we sit down and discuss the matter?'

'*Misérable*! Don't you "*Citoyen*" me.' He thumped his stick on his foot and gave a shout of agony.

I helped him to a seat in the sun, thankful that the surrounding buildings were a level lower than in the women's court, even permitting a glimpse of spires in the near distance. But the cobbles were hard under foot and dangerous when wet; and without so much as a colonnade for protected strolling, the rows of barred windows at every level created a grim atmosphere. It was not a comfortable place for an elderly gentleman to end his days.

Repressing a desire to remind him that his gout was self-inflicted, I mentally sorted through possible ways to alleviate his pain. 'I have with me a tea mix of yarrow and stinging nettles that could help. It must be made freshly and drunk several times in the day.'

'Hmph! Is't any better than your vile vinegar concoction that did naught but loosen my bowels and fill me with wind?'

I turned my gasp into a cough. 'It was meant for bathing your toes, not to swallow. Although it cannot have done you any real harm.'

The old man glared at me and I prepared to defend myself, if necessary, against the walking stick. And then he began to laugh. He flung back his head and roared, his wig tipping dangerously as he pounded his free hand against the seat. 'For my toes,' he wheezed. 'And I so bloated with gas that I might have wafted de Rozier's duck into the heavens without need for any balloon.'

I waited for him to recover, then apologized for not having made my directions clear. He'd have none of it.

Still chortling, he blew his nose on a fine lace handkerchief and waved aside the apology. 'In truth, the fault is mine. My temper is not equable, you may be surprised to hear, and I paid little attention to your words. This time I shall listen. The tea is to be taken internally and will not cause me to rise from the ground at irregular intervals, eh?'

'I cannot make such a promise,' I smiled. 'The workings of your internal organs are not clear to me. However, the tea will ease your pain; and I can give you some strips of white flannel soaked in castor oil to be warmed and wrapped about the toes for an hour, twice daily.' I turned serious. 'Indeed, I understand your suffering and can assure you of some relief, *cit*—'

'Don't say it! I will not have it.'

'*Tres bien.*' I rose, then bent to whisper in the old man's ear. 'Just this once … *Monsieur le Comte.*' And I went home with a lighter heart for the encounter.

Passing through the entrance hall I noticed a tall, dark man carrying a medical bag similar to my own. He was hurrying, intent on his goal, and didn't notice me, for which I was glad. There was no need to test my still precarious imposture against a colleague. No need at all.

CHAPTER 3

WAKING TO A crisp morning, with a sunbeam finding its way through the casement and across my bed, I felt a surge of well-being. Flinging off the coverlet, I danced across the cold floorboards to the washstand, arms flung wide and nightgown swirling about my ankles. This would be a day for me alone, my first wholly selfish day devoted to the happiness of Juliette Roussel since arriving in Paris. Sundays and saints' day holidays had been abolished and a new calendar was in place. Every tenth day was now declared a day off work, and this was a tenth day. People would be out and about enjoying the public gardens or boating on the Seine. I would join them.

After a hurried bowl of oatmeal, I dressed in shift and petticoats and looked through the few gowns stored in my chest. Red, white and blue would be a wise choice, but I didn't feel in the mood. I chose my favourite green bodice and jacket with the white skirt. No one would notice the stout boots of Docteur Roussel beneath the hem, boots designed to withstand the cobbles and muddy kennels of the streets. Brushing out my hair until it shone like copper strands, I piled it high, crowning it with a large green hat with a feather, and was ready to emerge as a woman once more.

On the way out I put my head around Mère Poisson's door and the lady laughed and clapped her hands, praising the beauty of the good doctor's 'sister'.

I bobbed my thanks, saying, 'There should be no need for my medical services. As for the Conciergerie, most prisoners scarce know one day from another and are not like to miss me.'

'You go, *petite chatte*. Enjoy yourself and I'll tell any one who comes that the *docteur* is not available today.'

'*Merci, ma mère*.' I blew her a kiss and trotted off towards the Rue du Faubourg Saint-Antoine in high spirits. It did feel peculiar to be without my breeches. I had to hold up my skirts to prevent them being befouled, and they interfered with my normal stride. Nor did I appreciate the comments and ogling glances of men as I passed by. I'd been the doctor's respected daughter in my village, and a man in the big city. Now I was being treated to city manners, or rather, lack of them, towards a woman alone in the street. All the same, I felt light-hearted and free of responsibility for the first time in weeks.

I missed the countryside with a longing that was almost a sickness, so today I headed towards the formal gardens of the Luxembourg. They were but a pale substitute, yet better than walls blocking out the sky. Traffic was heavy on the Saint-Antoine, both foot and wheeled, and I stayed close to the houses to avoid being jostled or splashed. The whole world seemed to be out enjoying this day, including Jaseur. I saw him pilfer an apple from a laden cart as the driver was manoeuvring around a heap of barrels fallen in his path. Half the street was blocked and running with brandy, and amidst joyful shouts and a roar from the unfortunate owner, people rushed to dip hands and cloths in the stream, adding to the confusion.

It was then I heard the sound of galloping hoofs and looked behind to see a carriage being driven at outrageous speed down the street, the horses wild-eyed and foaming under the lash, the driver half standing and wielding his whip like a madman. Behind him came a trio of horsemen in the uniform of the National Guard, sabres drawn, and coat-tails flying.

I flattened myself against the wall of a house, thinking in a split second that there was no room for this crazy driver to get through, that there would be a terrible smash amongst the broken kegs. And then it came, a cacophony of screams and snapping timbers, a whirl of plunging hoofs, and the awful shriek of an injured horse as the carriage ploughed through the blockage and turned over. The guardsmen reined in, dragging their mounts back on their haunches.

'Hold him!' shouted their leader. 'He's a damned *aristo* trying to escape.'

But I cared nothing for the driver who had been flung from his seat to land on a pile of squashed fruit and vegetables. I'd seen a small figure lying in the kennel, pinned by the body of a downed horse screaming and flailing the air in terror.

'Jaseur!' I picked up my skirts and ran. My heart pounded as if trying to escape my chest and I couldn't get enough air. I'd have flung myself down at his side, had not a pair of hands held me back.

'Wait!' a voice commanded in my ear. 'You will be kicked in the head.'

I paused, seeing that men had gone to the animal and were helping it to right itself, while another dragged Jaseur from within range of those deadly hoofs. As soon as he was clear, I pulled free of my captor and sank down amid the mud and rubbish and brandy dregs, my hands already sweeping the boy's body and limbs for damage.

The background shouting faded as I willed myself to concentrate on the messages travelling from my fingers to my brain. Jaseur lay still, eyes closed. All animation had gone from the vital little face. Then a shadow leaned over me and another hand, a finely modelled male hand, touched Jaseur's neck, feeling his pulse. I turned my head and saw the man I'd passed in the hallway of the Conciergerie a week or so earlier. His voice was deep and authoritative as he said, 'Let me see him. I am a doctor.'

I came so close to saying, 'So am I.' With no way of knowing whether this man was competent, I continued my examination and decided that, although Jaseur's arm was broken, his other limbs and torso had escaped injury. What concerned me most was his head. This doctor who had appeared out of the air had knelt down and was gently examining the skull and, I noted approvingly, taking great care of the boy's neck.

'Is he just unconscious from the fall?' I asked.

The man ignored me, and I suddenly realized he couldn't hear for the uproar going on all around. The bellowing of men, women and horses echoed between the walls of the houses. There were crashes and a fresh round of shrieks and then, above it all, a terrible, drawn-out scream.

I rocked back on my heels. '*Mère de Dieu*! What was that?'

'Don't look,' the doctor shouted, adding, 'The boy is not badly hurt, save for his arm.'

Relief washed over me and receded, leaving me feeling half-drowned but now able to breathe. Jaseur had become a part of my life since the day of his rescue. Restored to his usual vigour, he'd proved to be a scamp, yet I cared for him, as he showed in small ways that he cared about me, running my errands, singing my praises amongst his fellow urchins, even offering to fight anyone who said a word in my dispraise.

Another awful scream rose and died away in a bubbling moan. As I half rose, the doctor dragged me down by my skirt.

'Look away,' he bellowed. 'They are pulling that poor devil to pieces.'

I forced down the sickness rising in my throat and busied myself tearing my fichu into strips, while the doctor hunted amongst the debris of the vegetable cart for small pieces of timber suitable for a splint. Only the cart and the overturned carriage separated us from the bloody scene being enacted behind. My ears were filled with the ghastly sound of the mob, but in my head I was reciting every bit of poetry I could remember culling from my father's library. To the beat of iambic pentameter I steadied the broken bone of the forearm and, as soon as it was set and secured in a sling, helped pick Jaseur up and force a way through the crowd pressing in on that terrible scene.

At last we were far enough away to dim the voices celebrating murder. We came to a shabby café whose patrons had departed to join in the excitement and, with a brief word to me, the doctor carried Jaseur inside to lay him gently down on a banquette. Stripping his coat, he covered the boy, then beckoned to the hovering proprietor.

Protesting at the arrival of a brandy bottle, I said, 'The boy is still unconscious—' I found myself looking up into deep-set eyes of hazel flecked with gold – eyes that seemed to penetrate right to the heart of me, and capable of stripping away any pretence.

''Tis for you. You are suffering from shock,' said the doctor. 'And I intend to compensate my own nerves. Let us sit and gather ourselves until the boy recovers his senses.'

I realized how weak my legs felt, and gladly took the chair he pulled out for me. I also sipped at the brandy, knowing he was right. I *was* shocked, and glad of the warmth curling in my stomach as the brandy fumes filled my throat.

Now I was able to take stock of the man who had come to Jaseur's aid. I saw a tall, well-built figure, of perhaps thirty years of age, topped with an unruly head of black hair. His features were strong, rather than handsome, and those amazing eyes were sheltered by thick, frowning brows. This was not a man given to laughter and easy social converse, I thought. This man looked at life seriously, even sombrely.

He said, abruptly, 'My name is Armand Dumouriez.'

The name meant nothing to me, yet it was very clear that here was someone I could not afford to meet in my male persona. I'd have to be careful. I said, 'Then I must thank you, Citoyen Docteur Dumouriez, for your timely assistance.'

The heavy brows rose. 'The boy is surely not yours? Your younger brother, perhaps? No, of course not. You are of a different class entirely.'

'I am Juliette Roussel and Jaseur is a friend. His mother will be grateful to you, also.'

He brushed this aside. 'You seem to know a vast deal about the treatment of injured persons, Citoyenne Roussel. I should have expected the normal young woman to try to rouse the boy, to lift him, even to clasp him to her bosom.' I heard no sarcasm, only curiosity in his tone, and perhaps a touch of admiration.

I answered composedly, 'My brother is a Doctor of Medicine, *citoyen*, and he has taught me some of the basic principles. One does not move an injured person until satisfied that he or she has not damaged the spine.'

'Very true. You are to be commended for your level-headed-ness in an emergency.'

Now this was approaching condescension, and I had to suppress a retort. Steadiness in the face of disaster was not the prerogative of the male. Yet I felt that his plain speaking was habitual. He might even have meant to compliment me. Accepting it as such, I leaned over to check on Jaseur. His eyelids flickered and he began to sit up, but sank back with a cry of pain.

'Try not to move your arm, Jaseur. Lie there and rest a while before I take you home.'

Armand Dumouriez tossed off the remainder of his brandy and said, 'My carriage is nearby. The boy cannot walk in his condition.'

I almost laughed. A carriage in the Rue Bitone, an alleyway scarce wide enough for two cats to fight! 'You are kindness itself, *citoyen*, but we must not trouble you. I can help Jaseur—'

The frowning brows lifted and a most charming smile banished the last vestige of sombreness from his face. 'I must assume that my carriage would be too wide for the street. Then I shall carry the boy. You know you need help, and I'm quite accustomed to negotiating the maze that is the Saint-Antoine.'

I was reluctant, not stupid. Jaseur had been unconscious and was still very pale. If he faltered I could never carry him. And I need not reveal our joint address. Graciously accepting the offer, I declined more brandy and rose, watching the careful way the man handled the boy. With him settled against Dumouriez's shoulder, we set off together for Mère Poisson's house.

Of course, I should have reckoned on my landlady's reaction, a rush to clasp her child, and a torrent of questions and exclamations, amongst which she made it clear that I belonged in her house. Ah, well. My male incognito was still intact. I'd just have to make doubly certain not to cross paths with Doctor Dumouriez in my male guise. Hopefully, he wasn't a regular visitor to the Conciergerie. I'd certainly not seen him there before that one occasion.

Surprisingly, he accepted Mère Poisson's offer of coffee and one of her rock-like scones, and I was left tête-à-tête with him in the basement kitchen while Jaseur was fussed over and put to bed. I tried mentioning work and was reminded that it was a holiday. The doctor settled back in his chair and swallowed the unnameable brew in his coffee cup, clearly prepared to stay.

I wondered at this, deciding that it wasn't for my *beaux yeux*. Neither by look nor word did he show gallantry towards me. He just wanted to converse. Being relatively new to Paris, he had few contacts beyond one or two colleagues with whom he was not entirely in sympathy.

I ventured a question. 'Your work takes you to the Hôtel Dieu? I have heard … that is, my brother tells me his patients refuse to go there when they're sick. They name it a "death house".'

This provoked a lecture on the once great reputation of that hospital, which would be restored to its former glory when the Revolution was ended and a free democratic state achieved. He, Armand Dumouriez, would have a personal hand in its rehabilitation.

'Oh? You have large plans then, *citoyen*?'

'Indeed.' His squared jaw relaxed. I could see the moment when his particular daydream took over. 'France has always been famed for her advanced medicine. When we combine this with clinical instruction on the wards, as in the Vienna hospital system, when we elevate surgery to its proper rank and combine it with medical training, we will achieve the finest, most modern and successful model in Europe.'

So he was a surgeon. Even better. I was most unlikely to run across him in my work. Still, it was a pity we could have no professional discussions. While hesitant to display too much interest, I admired his certainty over the future. Only recently had the world begun to appreciate the difference between a barber who drew teeth and slashed off bits of offending flesh when not cutting hair and someone with years behind him of university study and practice in such centres of learning as the Vienna Allgemeine General Hospital.

This idea of an advanced twofold profession was an admirable purpose to aim for, although I could also see the pride behind the intention. Armand Dumouriez had a high opinion of himself. No false modesty there. Of course, there was no reason why he should hide his capability, or for me to entertain a fleeting, but strong desire to display my own.

I laughed inwardly at this unusual stab of competitiveness on my part. Where had it come from? Was I becoming so deeply embedded in my role that I must play the man, even in my petticoats?

As he was eyeing me curiously, I hastily assumed a suitably admiring expression and asked the kind of uninformed questions expected of a lay person. At least he judged me intelligent enough to comprehend the answers. How much I should have liked to meet him in my role as Dr Jules Roussel, a colleague. This man had a dream worthy of his passion and he knew how to present it for the admiration of others.

He stayed for an hour and proved an interesting conversationalist, ranging beyond medicine to the works of Voltaire, Leonardo and Mozart. And I, having had the freedom of my father's remarkable library, could meet him on common ground. Not once did either of us refer to the events of that morning. We both seemed to feel this fireside conversation was a brief escape from the misery and violence shading our daily lives. However, he finally rose to go, leaving instructions for Jaseur's care and thanking me for my company.

I bade him farewell with a strong feeling of regret and went upstairs to my room. By now I'd lost my holiday mood, so I put on my breeches and returned to work.

For some time I'd had in mind a scheme to help the unfortunate children imprisoned through no fault of their own. Today's episode, where an aristo had been responsible for the careless injury of a street child, had not shaken my resolve. The man had been fleeing for his life, and Jaseur had been unlucky to be in his path. But the high-born innocents suffering for the sins of their parents were just as unfortunate and deserved a chance to live.

The daring plan that I'd been developing was like a tree with multiple roots. First, there was my pity for the children wakening each morning to the knowledge that this might be their day to die under the bloody blade of the guillotine. Then there were the street urchins, ragged and half-starved under the old regime, and no better off now after crop failures and the food restrictions caused by the war. The aged and infirm suffered as well. Money would help the ragamuffins; courage and guile could save the little aristos. I hurried to the Conciergerie, anxious to begin.

The Marquis de Vergniaud-Chatelle dressed elegantly still. His amethyst coat of taffeta showed signs of wear, the lacing mended, the boned skirts limp and stained above ragged stockings, but he held himself with an air and greeted me with a flourish of his handkerchief.

'Ah, le bon Docteur Roussel. I give you good day, *m'sieur*.'

I nodded briefly. '*Citoyen*, may we speak privately?' I'd noted the anxiety he could not quite hide, despite the haughty curve of his painted lips. As he drew me aside I saw a knot of other lordly figures watching by the gate, their expressions disdaining a mere bourgeois in their midst. I said in a low voice, 'I've considered your request, *citoyen*, and I believe that something can be done.'

The marquis's jaw muscles relaxed. 'You will have my undying gratitude, *m'sieur*, if you succeed. 'Twill be dangerous.'

'Exceedingly dangerous, both for your child and for me, personally.'

'You are afraid?'

The words cut. 'Only a fool would not fear such an enterprise.'

My mild reply caused the man to react. He turned his head aside, muttering, '*Nom d'un nom*, I must be mad even to consider taking such a risk. If the guards should detect your piece of trickery—'

'There is a risk, but I would point out that mine is the greater peril. Your daughter is already under sentence of death.' I glanced back at the knot of men still idly watching, and at the guard who had strolled across to speak to them. 'Have a care, *citoyen*. If you arouse the slightest suspicion we are undone.'

The marquis drew himself up. 'You insult me, *m'sieur*. You may not question the behaviour of your superiors.'

I took a tight rein on my temper. If the scheme were not so important, for two deniers I'd have given it up. For a brief moment I savoured the words I longed to throw at this sneering elitist: 'Wherein lies your superiority, eh? You and your peers have behaved unforgivably. Your imperviousness to the suffering of the lower orders in their poverty and wretchedness is nothing less than inhumane. For too long have you been sealed away in your magnificent châteaux or in the gilded, hedonistic court without thought for these unfortunates. It should not surprise you to find yourselves where you are.' However, I said, instead, 'I believe I was the one insulted. However, we should set aside our differences if we are to succeed in saving your daughter.'

The man nodded stiffly and turned his back to the watchers. 'You have practised inducing this … this somnambulistic state in others, with success?'

'I have. And I have tested your daughter and found her to be a suitable subject.'

'Very well. Go ahead with the plan. I have had secret contact with *les clandestines* who will receive *mademoiselle* from you and carry her to my relatives in London. There remains only the matter of payment for your services.'

I shrugged. 'Costs are involved, *citoyen*, and my time is valuable.' Let him think what he would. There was no way I'd tell him his payment would go to feeding the guttersnipes whose existence he ignored.

I stood waiting until the man drew from his waistcoat pocket two diamond-studded shoe buckles and handed them over with a contemptuous look.

'Merci. *Citoyen*, I go now to speak to your lady and your daughter.' I bowed and moved away.

'*M'sieur!*'

I turned back at the sharp call.

'*M'sieur*, you will take every care?'

I bowed again, in answer, and strode off to meet the guard, a bawdy joke ready on my tongue to forestall any questions.

Half an hour later I was in the women's courtyard asking to speak with the former Marquise de Vergniaud-Chatelle, now simply Citoyenne Chatelle.

The marquise sat with her daughter, Louise, in a corner out of the wind, hemming a petticoat that by now would have done service for a scrub woman.

'*Bonjour, Citoyenne Louise*,' I greeted the girl. 'You are recovering so rapidly, I swear you have no need of a doctor at all.'

She smiled up at me. The thin cheeks were no longer flushed with fever and her eyes were clear, but she was thin as a birch broom. Her hair hung lank, and she huddled beneath a bed coverlet barely thick enough against the autumn chill.

'I pray you excuse us while I speak with your mama.' I nodded to the marquise, who rose and accompanied me a few steps away.

'What is it, M'sieur le Docteur? Is it her sickness?'

'No, nothing at all to do with that. She is recovering well. I have a proposal for you, *citoyenne*, which you might consider very carefully. It could mean your daughter's life.'

The marquise's hands went to her bosom. She was the picture of fright. 'What can you mean?'

I looked about me. Few of the prisoners cared to brave the gusty day and there was no one within earshot. 'I mean, that I might be able to smuggle Louise out of the prison and get her to safety.'

I thought the woman was about to faint. I grasped her elbow.

'*Citoyenne*! Take a hold of yourself. If you draw attention to us I can do nothing to help you.' I led the woman away from a smaller group near the fountain, then paused to add, 'Nothing is certain, you understand. However, with what is at stake, 'tis worth the trying.'

'Anything! Anything!' A sob broke the marquise's voice. I released my grasp, and she hunted for a handkerchief to dab at her face.

When she was calm, I explained. 'The first thing is, Louise must have a relapse. She must keep to her bed and I shall attend her daily until she is ready.'

The marquise said faintly, 'Ready?'

'Let us retire to your cell while I make clear my plan. If you agree to the proposal, I must swear you both to total secrecy.'

'You are mysterious, *m'sieur*.' A trace of the old arrogance had crept back into her voice.

'I've no desire to accompany you to the guillotine, *citoyenne*. If we make this attempt and fail, my head will roll with yours … and Louise's.' I was as emphatic as I could be.

The marquise capitulated. 'Your pardon, *m'sieur*. I swear that you will not be betrayed by me or my child. And if you can truly save her, I shall go happily to my death, praying for you with all my heart.'

CHAPTER 4

T WO DAYS LATER I returned, ready to put my audacious scheme into practice. When I showed the marquise and her daughter the medallion I proposed to use, the lady was charmed.

'A sweet conceit, *m'sieur le docteur*. I had one very like it as a girl. Of course, 'tis a memento of Madame Diane de Poitiers.'

I gazed down at the elegant little piece, remembering the day when Camille had given it to me as a memento and a farewell. A silver crescent moon was set on a swivel within a thin circlet of silver on a chain. When the chain was twisted, the circlet followed, while the crescent spun with a life of its own, gleaming with the brightness of a winter moon, flashing and dancing, dazzling to the eye.

The marquise looked up. 'How shall this ornament serve to help my daughter?'

'As a distraction, *citoyenne*. Please, listen to me without comment and you will soon understand.' However, it wasn't as difficult as I'd supposed to persuade the marquise that a practice similar to the art of mesmerism could be used to induce a semblance of death. It seemed both Anton Mesmer and the spurious Count Cagliostro had enjoyed the patronage of King Louis until ousted by genuine physicians. Their so-called magnetic 'cures' had been in vogue amongst the courtiers for some time prior to the uprising.

However, a cleverer man than either of the mesmerists, the Marquis de Puysegur, had gone on to devise a highly successful method of inducing artificial somnambulism. He'd trained its practitioners in his Paris institute until it was disbanded by the revolutionary government. My father had studied the technique and passed it on to me, and it was this sleeping trance that had eased Camille de Cassonnière's birth pains.

Now I proposed using it to give a child the semblance of death and spirit her out of prison.

Both mother and daughter were nervous, as was I, although hiding this beneath my professional demeanour.

'Is it truly possible to create the appearance of death?' wondered the marquise.

'I believe so.'

'And she will easily awaken?'

'Yes. When I say the words: "Awaken, Louise. Your sleep is over".' I had few qualms about the method; but my dependence would be upon the venality of hired bearers, and the capability of the aristos' secret organization, the *clandestines*, to carry out their part. Well, there was no going back now. I'd planned as carefully as I could, and it only remained to convince Louise that she should participate.

It turned out to be the main hurdle. Louise, naturally, didn't want to leave her mother, knowing her inevitable fate. The girl clung to her, weeping inconsolably, and I watched, feeling a helpless empathy that I dared not express. Having lost my own mother at an early age, I'd envied the evident bond between these two. Now I was witnessing the obverse of the coin of love, pain.

The marquise finally detached her daughter's clinging hands and held them while she spoke tenderly, yet firmly. 'Louise, you must have courage. There is a lifetime ahead of you if you take this chance.'

'I am not afraid for myself, *Maman*. 'Tis you I fear for.' Louise turned to me, her blotched face pleading. 'M'sieur le Docteur, you can save her, too. I beg of you—' She faltered, seeing my regretful expression.

'I am so sorry. I cannot. The authorities would suspect two deaths in the same family at the same time.' I could hardly add that I'd no intention of saving the aristos from the results of their own folly, even if it had been possible.

'Then I will not do it.' Louise sat back on her stool, hands tightly clasped, her face mulish.

'Louise!' The marquise's voice was a whiplash. 'You will obey me in this matter. Remember that you are a Vergniaud-Chatelle. We do what must be done, however high the cost.' Steely blue eyes met red-rimmed cornflower blue for a long moment, until Louise's gaze dropped.

Through lips stiff with the effort at control she said, 'I crave your pardon, *Maman*. It shall be as you say.' Her voice broke on the last word as she flung herself into her mother's arms.

I looked away to hide the moisture in my own eyes. For a moment I'd actually wished that I could save them both, even the marquise with her bred-in-the-bone superiority. Yet I knew this for what it was, a momentary sympathy that negated every-thing I believed and felt about the revolutionary battle convulsing society.

When I turned back, Louise had composed herself and the marquise had retired to the far end of the cell and disposed herself to watch. I picked up the 'Diane' trinket and held it before Louise's face.

'Shall we begin?'

It took less than one week. By the end of the fifth day it was certain that upon command, Louise would fall immediately into a tranced state resembling death far too well for the marquise's peace of mind. But she'd seen Louise awaken just as quickly and without any ill effect, whenever I gave the order. Initial maternal qualms had, by now, given way to an extreme effort to conceal her grief at the coming loss.

The chosen time arrived in a chilly late afternoon just before Christmas, when thickening clouds obscured the sun, sunk low behind the rooftops. The city seemed cloaked in a grey pall beneath which people scurried, head down, anxious to be off the streets.

The water in the fountain of the female yard was half frozen at the edge, dull and metallic looking. It was even gloomier in the prison cell where Louise, cradled in her mother's arms for the last time, was stonily silent, holding back tears with all her might so that her pale cheeks would not blotch and reveal signs of life. These had been powdered, and blue shadows skilfully applied. Her hair was lank, her body thinner than ever and so very cold. She'd lain for hours in the dank cell without covering, deliberately exposing herself in order to attain a properly chill and corpselike appearance. I felt great admiration for her stoicism.

The marquise looked up with tortured eyes as I said, gently, ''Tis time.'

Slowly Louise withdrew from her mother's embrace and went to lie on the bed. Everything had been said. The marquise bent and kissed her forehead, then retreated to her corner stool, her gaze never leaving her child's face.

Swallowing the hard lump in my throat, I knelt at the bedside and held the medallion before Louise's eyes. 'Watch it swing, Louise. Follow the moon as it spins, back and forth … back and forth, like a butterfly's wing fluttering, like a leaf swaying in the breeze … back and forth, first this way then that way, ever moving, spinning … spinning.' My voice grew softer as Louise's eyes closed and she listened to the suggestion that she would sleep, going deeper and ever deeper, until her breathing was slow and gentle, the air moving so slightly through her nostrils, her breast scarcely rising and falling, slipping ever deeper until she'd hear nothing, feel nothing, know nothing until my voice came to her, telling her to rise from the depths and awaken.

Eventually satisfied, I rose to my feet and turned to the marquise, an icy statue of grief immobile in her corner, saying, 'Have faith, *citoyenne*, and pray for us both.' I left to fetch the men who would carry Louise out on a board to the communal pit where all such remains were tipped and covered in lime.

Having folded the girl's hands, her mother stood watching as the stiff little body was loaded and carried out. Walking alongside, ready to steady the board if necessary, my heartbeat was a drum roll in my ears. This was the most dangerous period, when we must pass scrutiny by the officials. As the little cortège moved through the courtyard the women gathered on either side like a guard of honour, some quietly weeping. The male prisoners standing at the gates to their court removed their hats, some surreptitiously crossing themselves. One man dressed in an amethyst coat clung to the bars, his gaze riveted to the sad little procession. Then we were in the great arched hallway marking the principal axis of the prison.

'Halt! Who is in charge of this prisoner?' The clerk at his desk, flanked by two guards, pointed his quill at me.

'Doctor Roussel, the official medical attendant of the Conciergerie, and I have certified the prisoner as having departed this life one hour ago.'

'The prisoner's name?' barked the official, barely glancing up.

'The *ci-devant* Mademoiselle Louise de Vergniaud-Chatelle.'

The clerk entered the name in his book, then nodded to one of the guards, who stepped forward and poked a thumb in

Louise's eyeball. When there was no reaction, he stepped back again, grunting, '*Un lapereau mort.*' The clerk waved the men on.

Yes, just a dead young rabbit, I repeated beneath my breath, now that I could breathe again. We continued through the doorway leading to an outer yard. It was now nearly dark and a sharp wind nipped at my ankles beneath my long coat and lifted the 'corpse's' skirts. I longed to strip my coat and throw it over the pale form. However, I had to maintain the fiction until the two men bribed to open the gate had loaded their burden into the cart waiting nearby. They hadn't bothered to hide their ghoulish amusement at the thought of helping a grave robber to a tasty young corpse fresh enough for dissection. They'd been well paid. Why should they care? It was only one of those *sale* aristos who'd cheated the guillotine.

The job finished, they went off happily in the direction of the nearest wine shop, as cloaked and hatted men emerged from the shadows carrying a blanket. Swiftly, I wrapped Louise in it, murmured the awakening words in her ear. The girl stirred, looking up at her rescuers. One stooped to cradle her, the other took up the cart handles and, almost like magic, men and girl had melted into the darkness and gone. I stood in the wind for a long time staring after them, wordlessly praying for their safety.

I was relieved as much as elated. The cost in trepidation and moments of acute fear was far outweighed by the knowledge that a child was saved, and others would be drawn back from the brink of starvation. The plan worked, and it could work again. I could continue in the same way, carefully, circum-spectly, however fearfully, whenever opportunity arose.

On entering Mère Poisson's doorway an hour later I was the lighter of two diamond buckles, but with pockets stuffed with money. A loaf of bread was tucked under each arm, and I carried a bag of apples and a cheese, all of which were left at the doorway on the second landing. Behind this door lived a journeyman carpenter and his elderly parents, along with an invalid wife and five children, all subsisting on one man's wage, and forever pretending to be out when their landlady came looking for her money. At least they would eat tonight, and tomorrow I'd arrange financial help.

I sat down on my couch in the dark, with hardly the strength left to pull my boots off. The rescue of young Louise had gone well, but my initial elation had seeped away, leaving room for reaction. Trembling as with an ague, I could scarcely undo my coat buttons. My throat was dry as a kiln and so tight that my stock felt like a noose. I flung it from me and drank a great draught of water, with teeth chattering against the mug. And then I lay down and waited for the shaking to cease.

Slowly it did, and soon I was back to embroidering and extending my grand plan. Beginning with my fellow tenants, I hoped to spend some of the marquis's bounty on alleviating the worst cases in the district, and then hand the rest to a group of nuns who had been burned out of their convent during the September Massacres. These brave survivors had exchanged their lives of enclosure for running an open refuge for the destitute, and would put the money to the best possible use. As well, it was the Christmas season, and a time for sharing with friends and neighbours.

I was in the midst of arranging an employment scheme for some of my indigent neighbours when I fell into a deep, dreamless pit of sleep.

The following afternoon I returned to the women's yard at the Conciergerie to report on the success of the rescue mission. There the empty cell told its story. The *ci-devant* Marquise de Vergniaud-Chatelle had gone to meet her destiny.

Shocked by the narrowness of Louise's escape, I was tempted

to hasten into another rescue, but knew I must not. There were many reasons for circumspection, not the least being the need to deceive my 'corpse carriers'. Unlettered and generally unthinking, they were still likely to be puzzled over the need for a fresh body for anatomical study every week. And I didn't want to cause talk by seeking to hire new bearers every time. Gossip was the main pastime in our district.

Then again, I needed to coordinate with *les clandestines*, and could only do so through an aristocratic male prisoner. Which of them could be trusted? Which ones would trust me? Would the marquis, Louise's father be willing to help, or would he want nothing more to do with me, now that I'd served his purpose? There were still difficulties ahead, and haste could be fatal.

CHAPTER 5

A WEEK LATER in the men's section I overheard a guard jesting with his fellows about a prisoner who suffered such excruciating bouts of pain that he fell down and writhed on the stone pavement.

'*Regardez*. The kiss of *La Belle Guillotine* will cure him,' said one guard.

Another spat and muttered something filthy about how the man's disease had resulted from the bedding of aristo whores.

I stepped up to him and demanded the prisoner's name, which he gave in a surly tone. Clearly he regarded my job as superfluous. If the hated aristos were to die anyway, why tend them? I could have said something along the lines of common humanity, but knew it was a waste of breath. Too many prison employees were self-serving scum.

I entered Citoyen de Montsevre's cell hastily, and was over the threshold before realizing that the small room was full almost to overflowing. Too late, I recognized a tall figure bending over the prisoner, a grizzled man of amazing corpulence who was in the act of removing his pantaloons. Two others stood nearby like warders, as if about to pounce upon him. However, it was Doctor Armand Dumouriez who held my appalled attention.

Sang Dieu, but I was about to be exposed!

I saw his eyes widen and the look of astonishment, the quick reappraisal and the uncertainty. Without any real hope, I strode forward and presented myself in as deep a tone as I could manage. 'Good day, *citoyen*. I apologize for the intrusion, but I heard someone was in need of my services. I am Doctor Jules Roussel, medical attendant for the Conciergerie.'

The moment of truth was definitely upon me. That penetrating gaze stripped away my feeble pretence and hardened, and I braced myself for a verbal lashing. It didn't come.

Instead, Dumouriez greeted me in a steely voice. 'I am delighted to make your acquaintance, *Citoyen Docteur*. Your arrival is most opportune. As you see, at the request of the prison governor, I'm about to perform a surgical operation upon this man for a severe occlusion.'

I was bewildered. In what way was I opportune? And he'd obviously not been deceived by my imposture. Why had he not immediately exposed me as a fraud?

He continued smoothly, although I detected the anger beneath the surface, 'I should have informed you of my presence and my intention. Allow me to make amends for such discourteous behaviour and demonstrate to you a technique for saving the patient a long period of agony. You will find us a trifle crowded, I fear. Yet I beg that you will do me the honour of assisting at the operation.'

The man wasn't serious! I glanced back at the patient, to see him seated naked from the waist down in an elevated chair, his legs spread wide and his arms already pinioned by the other two men. And then I realized that this was to be my payment for what Armand Dumouriez saw as an outrageous mockery of his profession. I'd dared to lay untrained hands on the sick and the needy, as he thought. Now, trapped by my masquerade in a room full of males, I was to attend a lithotomy, the extremely painful and equally indelicate extraction of kidney stones through the male sexual organ.

The blood surged to my cheeks. I was startled, of course, but determined not to be provoked to a reaction. At the same time, I understood his attitude. To a doctor the patient is all important, and the idea that anyone, let alone a woman without proper training and qualifications, should risk lives was akin to sacrilege. Still, the situation was impossible.

With some effort I managed to sound a lot cooler than I felt. 'The prospect is most interesting, yet I fear I must decline. My services are required elsewhere.'

He held my gaze. 'You cannot refuse me a few minutes of your time. Your assistance could be both instructive to you as a medical man and invaluable to the patient in shortening the procedure. I'm sure that Citoyen de Montsevre will agree with me.' He turned courteously to his patient, who sweated with pain and apprehension and clearly didn't care who did what as long as they did it quickly.

Drawing in a deep breath, I reconsidered the situation. Perhaps it was not so impossible after all. I was trapped, yes. But I'd certainly seen people cut before, having assisted Father countless times in bleeding and cupping, in lancing boils and carbuncles. Nor was the male member unknown to me, at least on the page of a book illustrating a text, and most commonly displaying the oozing chancres of the pox. However, viewed in the quivering flesh, and in the presence of other men....

There was another consideration, the patient who suffered and trusted that he would be helped. My embarrassment was a small thing by comparison. This was the moment to display true professionalism and give aid to the very best of my ability.

I faced Dumouriez squarely. 'In that case, I am at your service. Please let me know just how I can assist.'

The heavy brows twitched, but if he was surprised, he hid it. Indicating the instruments laid out on a cloth, he pointed to one which might have been an invention for torture. 'This is the apparatus major which traditionally is used to dilate and incise the urethra and allow introduction of another instrument to extract the stone. The procedure can be a prolonged agony to the unfortunate patient and I no longer use it. Instead, I perform a lateral cystotomy, swiftly cutting through the perineum and opening up both bladder and bladder neck. The whole operation is over in minutes.'

'An improvement, indeed.' I understood the method he proposed, although he might not think so, and was impressed. If it did shorten the length of the ordeal, it must be applauded. He was an innovative surgeon and I looked forward to watching him and learning. I was pleased, too, to see that both he and his instruments were scrupulously clean, another departure from the norm.

An idea occurred to me. 'May I make a suggestion?' At his affronted expression I hastened to add, 'I do not presume upon your province, *Docteur*. I merely wish to advise you of a new treatment. I have in my bag a quantity of crystals derived from opium that produce a far better narcotic effect than laudanum. Also, if used properly and with caution, they have the property of killing severe pain.'

His tone was dismissive. 'Not the kind of pain that is the aftermath of surgery. There's no such anodyne. And I cannot experiment with some ... crystal ... of which I know nothing.'

Here an anguished voice broke in, 'Give it to me. I'll try it. But in the name of *le bon Dieu*, will you get on with the cutting?' It was the no-longer-patient Citoyen de Montsevre, shivering in his part-nakedness.

Dumouriez said over his shoulder, 'I'm about to begin, *citoyen*.' And to me, 'Might I ask you to pass instruments to me as I call for them; and perhaps you will assist me with the closure of the wound? 'Tis often slippery and hard to hold whilst tying off a ligature.'

Did he think I'd hesitate to have my fingers bloodied, or even faint at the sight of a gaping wound? No. I detected no sign of malice or prospect of enjoyment at my situation. He expected me to help, and I would do so.

The thick iron bars allowed little light to penetrate the cells, so an extra two candles had been brought in. In their flickering glow I stood beside Dumouriez as he picked up the knife, grasping the patient by his parts and dragging downward, and with his right hand drew the glittering blade across the taut-ened abdominal skin above.

Focusing on the capable hands and awaiting his request for assistance, I saw him slice surely through the layers down to the pouch of the bladder. And there were the stones, three of them lying like rough marbles in a cup. I shut my mind to the stifled screams of the patient, immobilized by his two supporters, and handed cloths and prepared ligatures, while admiring the swift precision of movement that ejected the stones, tied blood vessels and began to draw together the edges of the wound.

'Cautery would not be advisable here,' Dumouriez said, speaking as to a student. 'I incline rather to the application of a special wound salve I have developed, with a dressing affixed.' He straightened and glanced at the timepiece he'd laid nearby. 'Five minutes. Not as good as I had hoped.' Clearly he'd forgotten for the moment that I was not a student but an obnoxious, masquerading female.

I'd sweated along with the patient for every one of those minutes and had to comment. 'Speed is of the essence, according to any surgeon. I have heard it said that lithotomy can take as long as twenty minutes. Surely you decry your expertise.'

He said sharply, 'I challenge myself to improve my speed, to shorten the term of the patient's suffering.' He nodded to the two supporters to release de Montsevre, whose bitten lip bled sluggishly, and who struggled to hold back his moans. 'You two may go. You are not needed again until tomorrow.' He picked up the bottle of laudanum.

'Please.' I ventured to lay a hand on his sleeve. 'Whatever you may think of me, 'tis your patient who matters. I have the means to end his agony and allow him healing sleep. I beg you to try it.'

When he withdrew his arm, I knew that he would deny me. However, the moaning patient brightened. 'Give it to me, I pray you,' he begged.

Dumouriez looked dubious. 'I have no knowledge of the substance and cannot guarantee its safety.' He didn't have to add that without professional standing I couldn't be trusted to know what I was talking about.

Montsevre almost shouted, 'I will take the risk. Give it to me.'

Dumouriez threw up his hands. 'On your own head!'

I withdrew the pouch of crystals from my medical bag and measured the amount on to a set of tiny scales. This nostrum could depress breathing, and required careful and precise handling. From a bottle I poured alcohol into a cup of water and dissolved the minute amount of crystal, then handed it to the suffering man, who downed it at a gulp. Dumouriez looked on, frowning, without comment. But I had no doubts. I'd seen the miracle work. My only concern was that the pharmacist who had supplied the crystals might not agree to give me more, once this supply was finished. Or he might demand too high a price for it. However, while it lasted I'd use it to help conquer the agony that was inevitable with many diseases, and now surgery, too.

We helped the patient to his bed and stood watching as he drifted into sleep.

'Remarkable.' Dumouriez turned to me. I couldn't judge his

expression. 'And now, Citoyenne Roussel, I should like to hear an explanation of your curious and highly reprehensible conduct.'

Well, I'd expected this. It didn't mean that I accepted the censure meekly.

'Citoyen Docteur Dumouriez, I agree, an explanation is necessary. However, my conduct is not to be questioned. My father, an eminent medical practitioner, trained me for many years, and he believed me to be as competent as, and far more experienced than, any student to emerge from your famous universities. I have studied and learned to adapt to almost any circumstance, to be inventive and intuitive. I have saved lives, and, in my position at the Conciergerie, minister to the prisoners as well as any qualified doctor could do.'

'That is a matter of opinion. The impropriety alone—'

'What nonsense! We are speaking of competence, not the convenient, outmoded tradition that denies a female any role except subservience. I am intelligent, skilled and caring. And I only wear my brother's breeches because of the attitude of men like you.' I could feel my face heating as emotion boiled in me. It was all so unfair. I'd been doing so well until this unfortunate encounter.

The steely look in Dumouriez's eyes had gone, but his voice was cold as he responded, 'I grant that you mean well, and that you believe your training has been adequate. But what do you think would happen if just anyone claimed equality with a professionally trained doctor? Imagine the horrors that could be perpetrated upon unsuspecting patients.'

'It has happened in the past, and no doubt it still goes on. But your comments do not apply to me. You could test my competence and I'd pass the test because I have been well trained. I should have the correct qualifications if only the medical schools were open to women, which they will be, one day.'

His lips twitched. 'How militant you are. I cannot foresee a change of such magnitude occurring in my lifetime.'

'You are too sure, *Docteur*. The Revolution is bringing enormous changes to society. Already, women are taking a bolder place. It was women who marched on Versailles and took part in the attack on the Tuileries. Women are publishing in some of the journals, calling for representation in government and equality of opportunity.'

He said more mildly, 'I cannot deny that women are ill-served in the community. Yet the kind of upheaval you envisage is on such a scale as to disrupt society if it were introduced too suddenly. Over time we shall see the emergence of women in roles of importance, but not yet.' He paused and met my gaze as I sought to refute him. But I knew I could not. And suddenly I was tired of this exchange, leading nowhere. I needed to know where I stood at this time, not in years hence.

'What are you going to do about me?'

He was equally blunt. 'Nothing.'

He probably enjoyed my expression of disbelief, before adding, 'That is, I shall conduct an enquiry into the health of the remaining prisoners, and if they prove to have been well cared for, I shall not interfere with your appointment as their medical attendant.'

'Why? Why would you do this?'

'I'm not entirely sure. Perhaps I can sympathize with your position, after all. You have argued your case well, and I'm prepared to find that you are as competent as you say.' He shook his head. 'Perhaps it has to do with my feeling for *l'impartialité*. Those who aspire should be given their chance.'

I had to clear my throat before I spoke. 'Whatever your reasons, you have my gratitude.'

He nodded and returned to cleaning his instruments before replacing these in his bag. He pinched out the candles and added these to his baggage, still without further comment. I felt dismissed. Murmuring 'good day', I left more in the manner of a chastened student than a colleague, suspecting that this generosity had to do with the unimportance of the health of mere prisoners. But in my heart I knew I was as much a professional as Doctor Armand Dumouriez and one day he would have to admit it.

CHAPTER 6

T HIS UNFORTUNATE CONTRETEMPS preyed on my mind for the next few days as I moved between the sick and injured people of my section, that is, the new revolutionary division of the old city quarters, and the Conciergerie, snatching the odd meal of bread and cheese and onions. This was occasionally leavened with Mère Poisson's vegetable potage, in gratitude for regular payment of double the normal six sous rent per room per day. I enjoyed the cosiness of her basement kitchen with its worn but cared-for furniture. The pieces were quite old and had obviously been brought in at some time from a farmhouse. Whatever else had been sold for food, the heavy carved chairs and dresser had remained, mementoes of better times and, like the rotund Mère Poisson, were solidly comforting.

By now the money from the diamond buckles had disappeared like water poured into sand, sucked up by the great need of so many. I hesitated to take the risk of another rescue, despite the fact that Docteur Dumouriez had obviously decided I was fit to attend the prisoners. Then I was approached once again. Two weeks later, seven-year-old *ci-devant* Comte Jerome de St Villiers was pronounced dead amidst the wailing of his mother and sisters, and prepared for removal to the communal burial pit.

As before, I chose the end of a blustery day when prison officials would be warming themselves by a fire and paying scant attention to anything that drew them away from it. All went smoothly. The child's name was entered in the clerk's roll of death, and I stepped into the outer yard with the bearers, just in time to meet Doctor Dumouriez.

Everyone halted. My heart gave a great thump and my feet felt as if they'd stuck to the stones. But I strove to appear calm as I returned his greeting. The bearers stood as though petrified, their faces expressionless. I could almost hear the self-exculpatory phrases ready on their tongues: 'Nothing to do with us. Just doing our duty.' And if the worst happened, and they were accused of body-snatching: 'We thought he had a permit. It's only a stinking aristo he wants to cut up.' If they knew the truth, they'd be over the Pont Neuf in a twinkling and half-way across the city.

I thought of the *clandestines* waiting nearby and prayed that they'd do nothing rash. I'd get through this and get the child away. Just let the doctor move on about his business. I took one leaden step towards the gates. 'Forgive me, but we must hasten, *Citoyen Docteur*.' I motioned to the men to move on.

'One moment, if you please.' He barely glanced at the child, and turned to me. 'Could you not send the men to dispose of the body? I particularly wanted to speak with you, Docteur Roussel, about those remarkable pain-killing crystals.'

My brain seemed to have stopped working. I couldn't think what to do. Without my presence the *clandestines* would melt away into the shadows and my small charge would end in the burial pit covered with lime. But the man was insistent. Well, let him insist. I wasn't beaten yet.

With a warning glance at the bearers, I said, 'Your pardon, *citoyen*. I cannot do that. The child died in my care and, while the State denies him decent burial, I can at least accompany him to his last resting place.'

He looked surprised, as well as mildly annoyed. 'Commendable, although hardly a good use of your time.'

'The day is ended. Now my time is my own and this is how I choose to spend it. However, I'll willingly meet with you afterwards for a glass of wine. Shall we say at La Coquille within one half-hour?'

I thought he would refuse. The good doctor was clearly not accustomed to having his wishes denied. In the event, he bowed in acceptance, and took a step back. I wasted no time in ushering my bearers out the gates, and followed them without a backward glance.

My spine tingled with each step I took towards the alley where the *clandestines* waited. Would he follow? Why should he? Nevertheless, it took enormous willpower not to glance back over my shoulder, just to be certain.

The bearers tipped the boy into the barrow and departed without mishap, and I took up the handles and carried on. As I entered the mouth of the alley two shadows detached from the darkness. I gave the password and handed little Jerome over, whispering in his ear the words that would bring him back from the depths of induced sleep.

It was then I heard footsteps pounding along the cobbled street. A voice shouted, 'Halt, in the name of the Republic!'

As the *clandestines* melted away, I stepped out of the alley to face a group of National Guardsmen pelting towards me, sabres drawn.

I had to clear my throat before I could force out the words, 'Are you addressing me, *citoyen*?'

The foremost guard, an unshaven ruffianly type, peered into my face, saying suspiciously, 'Did you see them? Did they pass you?'

'No one has passed me since I left the Palais de Justice.' This sounded more important than the Conciergerie, which was just next door.

'They must be nearby. This was the place we were told.' His voice hardened. 'And who might you be, skulking around the prison after dark? Maybe you know more than you're saying.'

I drew myself up, cloaking myself in dignity. 'I find you offensive, *citoyen*. My name is Roussel and I am the doctor accredited to the Conciergerie, in charge of the prisoners' health.'

'So you say.' He turned to his men. 'We'll take him in and see whether interrogation will loosen his tongue.'

I was surrounded by naked blades. There was nowhere to go. Inwardly I quailed at the thought of an interrogation, possibly brutal, which would inevitably reveal my imposture.

Then a voice came out of the dark, a voice I recognized and which made my heart leap with thankfulness. I'd never thought to be so glad to see Armand Dumouriez.

'What is going on? What are you men doing?'

The captain of the troop responded automatically to the note of command. 'We're taking in a suspicious character. A party of aristos were informed on by a good patriot. They were supposed to be hereabouts, but we've lost them – probably warned off.' He jerked his head in my direction.

Dumouriez said coldly, 'Well, I hardly think that my friend and colleague, Docteur Roussel, will have anything to do with such matters. I am Docteur Dumouriez, officially attendant upon Citoyen Danton and members of the Revolutionary Tribunal.'

Every guard took a step backwards. The sabres were lowered.

'Then you vouch for this man, *citoyen*?' The leader was clearly disappointed, and not quite satisfied.

He was given no time to quibble. 'Unquestionably. And since you have lost your quarry, I suggest that you waste no more time idling here, but continue your search along the river bank.'

The leader turned on his men. 'Well, what are you waiting

for, *moutons inutiles*?' Their boots rang on the cobbles as they retreated. I could still hear their leader bawling at them in the distance.

The night was now bitterly cold, with wind driving the racing clouds across a moonlit sky. I shivered and drew my cloak tight, waiting for retribution to fall upon me. At least I'd saved the child.

Armand Dumouriez looked as though he'd like to hit me. I felt the impact of his gaze like a blow.

'*Idiote!*' he said. 'I half suspected a lie. Accompany a prisoner's corpse as a mark of respect! Of course, somehow the boy was kept alive, yet given the appearance of death, and he has now been spirited off.'

I shrugged, and looked away from those angry eyes. In the moonlight they had taken on a strange silvery hue, like the reflection off ice.

When I didn't answer, he added more roughly, 'You realize that, had I not seen the guards in pursuit and turned back, you would now be lost? How dare you take such a risk? Do you hold your life so cheap?'

I said, 'You would never understand. 'Tis over. There's no more to be said.'

'There is much to be said. I was the fool, to let you continue with your masquerade. I might have known that feminine emotions would undermine any pretensions to true professionalism.'

Pretensions! I choked on that. But what really enraged me was the accusation of feminine emotionalism. Never meek at the best of times, I thought there was little to be gained by restraint. I braced myself and told him what I thought of men who waged war upon children, of a Revolution that allowed scum to rise to high position, of a government that ignored the poor and the weaker members of the community. I got down to the particular and listed the families in my own building whose wage earners couldn't afford to feed them, and mentioned the sick and the abandoned living and dying in holes in a wall – all of whom had looked to the Revolution to bring them salvation. 'So that is what I think of your great social experiment! A failure, dragging our country into war and leaving its people in worse case than when living under the heels of the aristos.' I drew breath and felt the fury leaching away, leaving me colder than ever.

There was a silence. Then he answered, quite mildly, 'There is merit in your accusation. Yet I fear you lack a full under-standing of the Revolutionary process, which must first pull down before it can rebuild.'

'Well, I have seen more than enough of the destruction.' I couldn't be bothered to argue further. Why *were* we arguing over opposing viewpoints when my world had come crashing down? Why didn't he get it over with?

He was still making his point. 'There will be many places and people brought to ruin before the end. You need to grasp the total plan. You need—' He gave a sudden gasp, and I realized that he was struggling not to laugh. '*Nom d'un chien*, but you have a way of turning things upside down. You dare to chastise me when you have been busily undermining the law in the Devil only knows how many ways.' He took me by the shoul-ders and stared down at me, as if to impress his words deeply. 'By rights, you should be denounced, but I find I cannot do it. However, you must not continue to flout the law and support the enemies of the state. Will you give me your *parole d'honeur* not to attempt any more rescues?'

That wasn't worth a moment's thought. Although the *clan-destines* might be wary of working with me again, somehow I'd find a way to continue saving innocent children. Pulling away, I looked him straight in the eye and said, 'You have my word.' And of course, being a man, he believed me.

I felt no remorse, only overwhelming relief.

He released me, saying, 'Good. You know, this grand experiment is being carried out for you, and for every man, woman and child in France. You feel disenchanted with it at the moment, but to have thrown off the yoke of tyranny is a great step. In time, great changes will come and all will benefit. Will you accompany me to a meeting of the Cordeliers Club and learn what this Revolution is really about?'

I gave this request some thought. It wasn't so very much to ask. He had been most generous towards me, and despite all that was at stake, I was aware of a small itch of guilt over lying to him. 'Very well. I shall try to keep an open mind. But neither you nor any of the speakers at your club will sway my opinion.'

He looked pleased. 'That will be seen. Now, may we please go somewhere out of this ferocious wind? I'd like you to tell me more about the properties of the pain-killing crystals.'

Members of the Cordeliers Club, formally the Society of the Friends of the Rights of Man and of the Citizen, had originally met at the nationalized monastery of the Cordeliers, not far from the dreadful prison where Jaseur had almost lost his life in the September Massacres. They now met at the Salle du Musée, close by the Conciergerie. I accompanied my forceful colleague to the meeting that week, with every expectation of a thoroughly uncomfortable few hours ahead of me. This most democratic of all the political clubs had a reputation for stirring up violence, and its members were totally opposed to the monarchy.

Armand was an enthusiast. 'This is the one club with unrestricted admission, claiming that men and women of all classes constitute the sovereign people.'

'They admit women?'

'Certainly. They are some of the more vocal members.'

I was about to suggest that I should attend as a woman. It

would be an opportunity to enjoy my true role in public. He seemed to read my thoughts.

'It would be best for you to retain your male attire. You are too obviously of a certain class and would draw attention in such company. Unlike the Jacobins, the members are predominantly workers, although with a fair proportion of the bourgeoisie represented. The male bourgeoisie, you understand. Until recently, George Danton was one of the more influential leaders. Lately, however, he hasn't appeared at the meetings. He's most likely too concerned with the war, and leaves the others to watch over the Revolution at home.'

To me this sounded ominous. 'How do you mean, "watch over"?'

'Why, to guard against the danger of counter-revolution; to strike out against the speculators and food hoarders; generally to watch over Paris itself. Come and listen and you will understand.'

I said no more. I'd promised myself that no matter how much I disagreed with what was said, I would behave circumspectly as a guest at the meeting. Armand could so easily have denounced me as treasonous, yet twice he'd let me go. It was astonishing, given his deeply entrenched belief in the Revolution and his hatred of the old regime. Perhaps he had a fondness for children. He'd certainly handled Jaseur gently.

As we blended with the crowd in the meeting room, I was interested to see that most were dressed soberly in the costume commonly associated with members of the Third Estate, that is, in plain, dark coat and breeches and even plainer shirts. There was a smattering of men in wigs and splendid court dress, and several wearing the Jacobin costume of blue sleeveless waistcoat and white sailors' trousers topped with the red Phrygian cap. A democratic assembly, I thought, and probably representative of the mass of the people.

Then I saw a man thrust through the crowd and on to the podium. He was the strangest figure, dark, intense, with wide-set, greenish-yellow eyes and a long, twitching mouth. His whole body seemed to twitch as he leaned forward to speak, his grubby shirt open to reveal an ugly rash, and a red bandana tied around his greasy, matted hair.

I whispered to Armand, 'That man is ill. He has open sores on his face.'

Armand looked uncomfortable. 'Oh, Marat. I really believe he is half mad, with his diatribes in his news journal and his desire to kill all those opposed to his beliefs. Still, one cannot doubt his courage, or his importance as a propagandist.'

'But the sores. Surely he could be treated—'

'They are his flag of independence. He contracted a horrible skin disease whilst hiding from the authorities in the sewers a couple of years ago. He has always been in trouble. Now he simply lives for the Revolution, nothing else.'

I shuddered as the harsh voice rose, ranting against the enemies of the State, denouncing the members of the right-wing Girondin party and calling for the monarchy to be wiped out. To my surprise, this was greeted with loud cheers. And when he finally stepped down, his place was taken by another member who immediately broached the subject of the king's punishment.

'This Louis Capet, this Monsieur Veto, this drunken drip is about to be tried before the Convention and found guilty of treason against our country. The people will demand his life in payment. 'Tis our duty, nay, our imperative to vote for the death penalty.' Even louder cheers followed.

I paled at these words and swiftly scanned the nearest faces. They were all alive with the kind of avid excitement I'd seen in boys on a rat hunt. When this speaker made way for others, the same sentiments were repeated with variations in style, yet with equal intensity.

I turned to Armand, my good resolutions forgotten. 'Is this why you brought me here, to listen to regicides?'

He, too, had paled, but his answer was firm. 'They are right. We can have no true democracy while the king lives as a rallying point for the monarchists. The Revolution is endangered from within, as well as being under attack by other nations. This is no time to display weakness of purpose.'

'Hear, hear.' A fair-haired young man standing nearby clapped appreciatively and turned to me. 'Marat knows the Girondins are royalists at heart. They, and the king, must be destroyed. Liberty must prevail at any price.'

'And blood must be the price?' I shot at him. My rising anger threatened utterly to wipe out my good intentions. How dared Armand bring me to listen to such a rabble spouting their hatred and blood lust. He called this patriotism! He must be as mad as Marat.

The fair-haired man eyed me curiously. 'Blood is always the price of freedom. We must kill to cure.'

'No! Never! You should be working to win over minds and hearts, not cutting off heads. If you kill the king you will bring down the execration of the world upon France.'

The man's face darkened. He held up his hand when Armand would have intervened. 'So, do we have here a sneaking royalist? Would you return the traitor and his Austrian bitch to the throne?'

There was a murmur from the men standing nearby.

Armand stepped to my side, saying, 'Leave be, Saint-Just. The lad is a doctor trained to save lives, not take them. And he is politically naive. I brought him here tonight to show him the reality—'

This was too much for me. I felt the blood rushing to my head as I rounded on him. 'Your club is nothing but a haven for a pack of cut-throats, *citoyen*. All I've heard tonight is a call for violence and blood-letting, and nothing about the real problems facing us: the war, the lack of food, the failure of the State to provide adequate services to the people—'

Saint-Just spun me around and grasped the front of my coat, dragging my face almost into his. '*Pardieu*. You will swallow those words, *fomentateur*.'

'Let him go.' Armand wrenched me free, leaving several coat buttons behind. He held me against him momentarily. Then Saint-Just grabbed at me again. I saw the glint of red in his eye as he tried to drag me away towards the podium, encouraged by those who had heard their exchange.

'Traitor!' yelled a voice. 'Malcontent!'

'Nonsense, he's a mere child,' said another.

I struggled to pull free, angry and frightened and, above all, shocked at being manhandled. 'Let me go!' I kicked out at my captor's shin.

He let out a howl and swung his fist at my temple and I collapsed to the floor.

'Shame,' called someone, while others laughed.

'*Sacré*! Are you hurt?'

I heard Armand's voice through a whirling darkness and felt him lift me to my feet, keeping an arm about my shoulders. Somehow I stumbled to the door as the jeering crowd parted before us. My legs threatened to buckle and I was glad to sit on a bench in the entrance. My hat had fallen off and I laid my head back against the wall and closed my eyes. Dimly, I heard Armand swearing softly to himself.

What a mess, I thought. And I'd brought it on myself. Why had I spoken out? My unruly tongue had brought me trouble, as it had so often in the past. As Father always said: too much of my mother's red hair and a fair amount of her temperament.

I opened my eyes and saw by my companion's attitude and expression that this was the end of all social intercourse between us. I had publicly embarrassed him, perhaps even tainted him with my own supposedly treasonous outburst. In his eyes there'd be no greater crime.

I grasped my hat and forced myself to my feet, saying, 'I am unhurt. But I believe I should return home. I pray you forgive this disturbance and return to your meeting.'

He said, abruptly, 'I'll accompany you to your lodging. 'Tis late and you are unwell.'

My head ached and I was not in the mood for male high-handedness. 'Citoyen Docteur Dumouriez, I need neither your help nor further interference. I do not like you, or your friends, or your politics and I hope never to cross your path again.'

It was enough. He turned stiffly and re-entered the club, and I walked off towards the bridge.

CHAPTER 7

I T WAS A typical January night, cold enough to keep people off the streets. Moonlight shone on icicles hanging from windowsills and eaves, and the chill rose through the ground and through the soles of my boots. I was miserably conscious of feeling ill, probably from the fright of experiencing personal violence. For the first time since coming to Paris I was lonely. There wasn't a soul in the whole city, save for my landlady and her son, who would care whether or not I ever returned to my lodging.

I indulged this melancholy thought as I trudged across the bridge and headed for the maze of courts and alleys of the Saint-Antoine quarter. It was a long, weary way to the Rue Bitone and my bed under the sloping roof of *chez* Poisson. I quailed at the thought.

At the sound of footsteps behind me my overwrought nerves immediately sprang to action. I was being followed! Was it footpads? Was I possibly going to end the night in the gutter, half-dead, or worse, as a corpse floating in the Seine? I forced my legs to a shuffling run, and the footsteps increased their pace. My heart pounded so loudly I was deafened. Melancholy had fled and now jagged flashes of fear spurred me to greater speed. I wished that I had skill with a rapier. I wished for a pistol. How I wished I was safely at home out of this bitter night. I stumbled and regained my balance, feeling a cramp in my side, yet forcing myself on.

'Wait! Please. I wish to speak with you.' The voice was close behind me, and the accent was definitely not that of a Frenchman. But it was an educated voice, with no hint of a threat.

My jangled nerves quietened and I slowed and turned. A tall, slim figure stood revealed in the light of a street corner lantern. He was dressed fashionably in sober style and was not threatening in the slightest.

'*Citoyen?*' I gave myself time to regain my breath.

He swept his tricorne hat most elegantly. 'Peter Lombard, at your service. I ask pardon for frightening you, but you moved away so swiftly.'

Frightening me? He surely would not say that to a man. A horrid doubt had crept up on me, and I said as stiffly as if outraged by the inference, '*Citoyen*, you are mistaken.'

'Oh, I think not. I witnessed the contretemps at the Cordeliers Club, and your collapse and the attitude of your companion told the tale. You are a woman, are you not? I may say, a very courageous woman who speaks her mind.' His smile was pleasant, yet I remained wary. He had an open face with regular features, and a head of thick hair whose silvery hue would be fair by daylight. And his courteous manner could not be faulted.

I answered slowly, 'You are perspicacious, *citoyen*, and I think, a foreigner?'

'English. I am visiting your country out of curiosity. 'Tis not every day one may witness the workings of a social upheaval. I am as inquisitive as a cat.'

English. That explained it. Everyone knew the English were an unpredictable race ruled by a mad king. Even so, his behaviour required an explanation. 'Why did you follow me?' I asked.

'Why, to see you safe. You were knocked half unconscious and then abandoned by that … by your companion.'

'He had good reason to be angry. And I dismissed him.'

'Nevertheless, you should not walk alone. You will permit me to escort you?'

I hardly knew what to say. At the rate things were moving, my secret life would soon be on display for all the world to see. Yet the blow to my head had weakened me, and it would be a relief to have some support, should my legs fail. The man did seem determined. It was an annoying male characteristic.

I decided to trust this Peter Lombard. 'Your company is welcome, *citoyen*, although I fear you will find my lodgings are at some distance, and in an insalubrious quarter.'

'*De rien, mademoiselle*. T'will be an honour to accompany you.'

His accent really was execrable! But such kindness as his was not to be disdained. I was glad to lean upon the arm he offered, most particularly when negotiating the unlit lanes of the Saint-Antoine. Between the darting rats and the rubbish and the odd raised cobbles, the danger of a broken ankle could be very real. The journey passed quickly. He didn't tax my poor aching head with questions, remaining silent for the most part, except when requiring directions. And having delivered me to my doorstep, he lingered only to ask permission to call upon me at another time.

'I have mentioned my insatiable curiosity,' he reminded me. 'I long for an explanation of your masquerade. You may believe that I would never betray you.'

I did believe him, even upon such short acquaintance. After all, what would it profit him to report me to the authorities, who were the only people likely to be interested? Besides which, if I fobbed him off he might try to follow me some day and inadvertently betray my secret. So I thanked him for his kindness and promised to have supper with him at a certain café on the next tenth-day holiday.

Climbing into bed, I reviewed the evening's events, admitting my regret at having cut all ties with Armand Dumouriez, and in such a manner. I admired the man's skill and devotion to the betterment of his profession, and the care he'd displayed for the well-being of a street urchin. I liked his straightforwardness and was grateful for his forbearance towards me. Yet I loathed the system he supported. His politics were tainted with bloody violence, and I could never understand or enjoy friendship with such a person. I told myself firmly that I was well out of such a disturbing relationship.

A few days later all thoughts of my own situation were eclipsed by a truly awful event, the trial and execution of the King of France.

I'd known he was facing his accusers before the Convention, and waited with the crowd milling outside the building to hear the verdict. It horrified me. Bombarded on all sides with shouts of approval, I went home, promising myself that I would honour the condemned monarch by attending his execution.

Later, without the heat of outrage, I reviewed my decision. Accustomed as I was to the sight of blood and the pain and misery of others, I'd be exposing myself to an emotional upheaval far beyond the usual necessary professional distancing. But I was angry. This man, this king who had tried to govern to the best of his ability, was being made a scapegoat for the sins of a whole sector of society. How many, watching him die, would express any kind of compassion or understanding? I could answer that question. There would be at least one. I could bear witness to his passing and honour the courage I knew he would display. He was, after all, a monarch.

So, on a grey, drizzling morning I duly made my way to the Place de la Révolution, hearing the distant drumming as the king's carriage approached.

The streets were lined with National Guardsmen and citizens

armed with muskets and pikes, while the square itself, with the grim scaffold at its centre, was jammed with sightseers. Pushing my way through with determination, I ignored the curses and jostling and climbed a flight of steps, clinging to a railing to see over the heads in front of me. The drumming grew louder, the beat increasingly ominous, accompanied by the sound of marching feet. The guards came into view, their white bandoliers and cockades catching the sunlight, and behind them the royal carriage.

My throat grew tight and my eyes moistened as I saw the short figure descend, unassisted, shaking off the men who tried to remove his clothes. When he was down to his waistcoat, he was bound, protesting the indignity, and his hair cut off. Now bare-necked, he climbed the steps of the scaffold; all the while the drums beat ominously.

I felt those drumbeats in my blood. They ceased briefly to let the king address the crowd: 'I forgive those who are guilty of my death, and I pray God that the blood which you are about to shed may never be required of France—' His next words were drowned out as an officer shouted a command to the drummers, who resumed the beat. The king was seized by the executioner and laid down on the plank of the guillotine.

I tried to look away as the plank slid forward. Then I reminded myself of why I'd come to this place – to bear witness. And so I did. The rope was pulled, the blade descended and the king screamed. It took another stroke to sever his neck. When the head was held high by a young officer, strutting about the platform to show it to the people, with accompanying crude gestures, I turned away at last, revolted to the very core. Voices rose around me, fierce with joy: 'Vive la Nation!' 'Vive la République!' Hats were thrown in the air. The guard of cavalry waved their helmets on the points of their sabres, and people rushed forward to dip handkerchiefs or pieces of paper in the blood spilled on the scaffold, as mementoes of the event.

I fought my way to a drain and was sick.

Nevertheless, I was glad I'd been one of the few who stood there for him, silently applauding his composure and courage. I knew I'd seen the beginning of a terrible chapter in my country's history.

I had been right, too, about the howl of execration going up all over Europe condemning the 'heinous crime' of regicide. Within a few weeks France was at war with almost every major power, including England.

One evening when I could feel the touch of spring in the air, I closed the door on the last patient and changed into my second dress, ready to dine out. My patients that day had been the usual run of broken bones, sad-eyed children with all the ills of starvation, and an interesting man whose symptoms of abdominal pain with vomiting and bleeding had finally brought him to seek help. I observed several other indicators pointing to poisoning, and wondered how to broach the possibility that someone close was helping him into the next world.

Like almost every person I saw, he 'knew' the trouble, and the likely cure.

I said, 'Citoyen Ferrier, I do not believe in any crab eating away at your guts. Nor will a dose of the black peppermint laced with laudanum do anything for you.'

Ferrier shook his grizzled head and clutched at his stomach. His face was grey with pain and his eyes pleaded with me to do something.

What was it my father had drummed into me? Examination, palpation, listening, comparing and questioning. What questions had I not asked? 'Citoyen Ferrier, what work do you do?'

He answered with some pride, 'I'm a copper foundryman – have been these seventeen years.'

I sat back. 'Therein lies your problem. You are working in a field where arsenic is used, and over the years you have inhaled the fumes and had the dust lie upon your skin. You are being poisoned by your work.'

Naturally, he didn't want to believe this. By the time he'd left with something to soothe his pain, he was still in a state of denial. There was nothing I could do to convince him that he was killing himself, and there the matter rested. I locked away my drugs and potions and set off for the Café Bearnaise and my supper companion.

Peter Lombard remained in Paris, despite the facet that his country was at war with the French and, even while remaining discreet, he somehow managed to cross my path continually. He frequently joined me for supper to discuss the day's events. The son of a mine owner, he had a commendably altruistic interest in the health of his employees, plus his admitted curiosity, and he made it clear how much he admired my devotion to my work. He also clearly admired my person, which was flattering but awkward, in the circumstances. I liked him for his openness and for his abhorrence of the Revolution's excesses. However, the liking had not grown into a more tender emotion, and I kept him at a distance.

There was also the fact that, against all inclination, I continued to measure him alongside another man – an opinionated, exasperating man who, nevertheless, occupied my wayward thoughts.

The café was clean and well lit, the scuffed timber floor filled with narrow-legged chairs and tables covered in actual linen, patched and frayed, but hardly stained at all. The place was positively palatial, for the Saint-Antoine quarter. Peter greeted me with obvious pleasure, seating me as ceremoniously as if I were decked in diamonds and of royal blood. He had ordered my meal and wine and now proceeded to flatter me with comments upon my appearance.

Father had never socialized with his neighbours, which meant that my wardrobe had always been strictly utilitarian. My mother's blue velvet gown was one of the few mementoes I possessed. It was so dated that I'd been forced to hack off the hampering train, and I quite failed to fill the bodice beneath the hastily tacked in fichu. However, Peter, found no fault with it, or with me. I accepted his compliments with an inward smile and hoped to move him on. He remained conventional, asking after my work day, praising where he could. Not a word about himself, I thought. How gentlemanly. How thoughtful. How … bland.

At last I succeeded in steering him away from the personal, and his innate curiosity then led us into more absorbing pathways. He was particularly interested in medical innovations.

'This Peruvian bark brought in by sailors, you say 'tis good with fevers?'

I shook my head. When I'd swallowed the mouthful of excellent *pot au feu* I answered, 'Although 'tis thought by many to be a cure-all, I believe it works only with the intermittent ague arising from the swamps. Unfortunately, it not only tastes vilely bitter, but induces vomiting and purging, so 'tis unpopular with patients.' I sighed. 'I did once hold in my hands the most magic of opiate crystals which relieved pain and induced healthful sleep. But the man who knew their source has disappeared. I fear that he is one of the latest victims of this bloodthirsty Republic.'

'Hush!' Peter looked around the tables. However, the café wasn't well patronized and there was no one near enough to overhear. Peter would have had me dine in style in a place like the Palais Royal, but I was more comfortable in my everyday milieu. I'd not yet come to terms with the extreme contrasts between the aims of the Revolution and its results. Vast numbers of citizens still carried on as usual, immune to the misery of so many, heedless of the bloodletting taking place in the name of brotherhood. It would have choked me to dine in the company of such uncaring people.

Now Peter placed his hand over mine on the table. The blue eyes beneath their fair brows were intent upon me. 'You make me fearful, Juliette. You are too outspoken for the times.'

'Only with you, Peter. Remember, most of the time I am a man, and perfectly circumspect.' I withdrew my hand.

'I remember, only too well.' He sounded rueful. 'I wish you were out of this masquerade and back in your petticoats permanently. Then I might address you in the guise of more than friend.'

I frowned. 'No more, Peter.' My tone warned him not to persist with this line of conversation. The truth was I valued his companionship too much to risk letting it spill over into maudlin sentiment. There was no one else with whom I could be myself. If that was selfish, then I'd plead guilty to the sin, and continue to use Peter as a buffer against the pain and despair of others that coloured my working days and sometimes crept into my dreams.

Another man might have refused to be silenced. A different kind of man, more forceful, more passionate. Someone more in the mould of the opinionated Doctor Dumouriez. Dear Peter, so kind and so unlettered in the ways of the opposite sex, retreated, as I knew he would.

He sat back. 'Oh, very well. Let us return to your profession. 'Tis your belief that much disease is caused by contagion, far more than the common pox and, of course, the prison fever, the typhus?'

'My medical confreres tend to blame poor physical stock, or bad lifestyle for most disorders, when they are not adhering to the outdated miasmic theory.' I smiled without humour. 'I, on the other hand, try to seclude someone who is coughing up sputum from the white plague of the lungs. I tell the mother of a child with the film growing across his throat not to kiss him upon the mouth and to keep the other children from him. For he will surely die. Yet his siblings need not. Sometimes they heed me; more often they block their ears. And of course, they live in such crowded conditions.'

I'd learned to ignore the bruising to my heart as I watched these innocents suffer and die. Yes, at times the ignorance of their parents was at fault. But more often it was poverty and starvation that warped them out of shape and doomed them from the day of birth. Those who did survive infancy still ran a terrible gauntlet of disease and deprivation, and I could do so little for them.

I thought also of the children I tended in the Conciergerie, keeping them alive for the executioner, and mourned the futility of it. As with the street waifs, I could save so few. The breach with Armand Dumouriez had helped in a way. I'd asked to be informed whenever he planned to visit the prison, and he, naturally assuming that I wished to avoid him, complied. With this advance warning I could be sure he'd not catch me out in my lie. Fortunately, the *clandestine* organization had not abandoned me, simply changing their route and disposing of the informer within their ranks.

Peter said, 'You give so much to your little patients. I see how they love you, even the wildest of urchins. As for young Jaseur, I think he has adopted you.' His smile lit features quite ordinary in repose. Blue eyes sparkled and suddenly he was *gamine*, like one of the street children.

'Jaseur is special,' I admitted. 'He likes you, too. Perhaps because you play at hand-ball with him and his street friends, and treat the winners to pastries.' I drained my glass and rose. 'I must go. I have a mother expecting to deliver at any moment and I must change and be ready for the call. 'Tis her fifth pregnancy, poor woman, and none of the infants has lived. God send this one survives.'

He grasped my hand, preventing me from leaving, and I realized that his compliance had been momentary. He insisted upon opening his heart to me, after all.

'Juliette, you must let me speak. I do so admire and love you. I wish you would let me take you away from danger, to England, to my home.'

I jerked my hand away, disturbed by his intensity. The look in his eyes was almost frantic. He must really be worried about me. But it would not do. I had to make him see reality, even if it cost me his friendship.

'Peter, I am honoured that you should care for me in this way. However, I could never abandon my calling, or my children. They need me, all of them.' I could almost see him damning the children in his mind. Fond as he was of them, clearly his concern for me took precedence. While he struggled to find the right, persuasive words, I added, 'If you cannot forget this and continue to be a friend only, then I will not see you again. I do value our friendship, very much, and would be sorry to sever it. Yet I will, if you do not see reason.'

He capitulated, or appeared to. However, I knew he hadn't given up hope, and I was sorry. There'd come a time when the strain between us would be too great, and that would end our relationship. Peter needed to leave Paris, to return to his own country and people. I must, somehow, persuade him of this before it was too late.

CHAPTER 8

ONE AFTERNOON, FORTUNATELY not a day upon which I was engaged in child smuggling, Armand waylaid me at the entrance to the Conciergerie. I was shocked that my warning system had failed and waited in some trepidation for him to speak.

He was unusually mild, not retiring of course, but clearly displaying a spirit of reconciliation. He even addressed me in the polite plural form, now outlawed in an attempt to equalize all citizens in every walk of life.

'*Bonjour*, Citoyen Docteur Roussel. *Comment allez-vous?*'

'I am very well, thank you. And you?'

'Well, also. And your charges?'

We danced around verbally until he at last came to the point.

'My friend, George Danton's wife is sick unto death, and suffering appallingly. I hope … that is, could you possibly visit her and administer a dose of the liquor you make from the crystals?'

It must have cost him to beg a favour of me, yet he hadn't hesitated when the good of a patient was involved. Or, if he had, he hid the struggle well.

I said, quite cordially, 'I have only a very small amount left, although sufficient, I'm sure, to help Citoyenne Danton. When would you like me to come to her?'

'Now, if you could. Danton is away at the front lines, but he trusts me to give Gabrielle every aid. He will be here shortly, although I fear he will be too late to bid her farewell.'

I could see that he grieved for this Gabrielle and felt an odd stab somewhere near my breastbone. I told myself it was natural for him to care for his friend's wife, who was also a friend, and I agreed to come at once. It felt strange to be sitting beside him in his carriage, and at first our conversation was stilted. However, by the time we arrived at *chez* Danton we had reached an understanding. I had accepted an unspoken apology for the events within the Cordeliers Club on that unforgettable occasion, and I let him understand, without precisely saying so, that I'd spoken hastily and wished to withdraw my words of dismissal. All the same, our differences lay between us like a chasm with only the flimsiest bridge for crossing. And we both knew we should tread this bridge with the greatest care.

I wasn't surprised to find that the Dantons lived in good style. There was a great deal of the sybarite in Armand's friend and it showed in the costly furnishings of his home. I was particularly taken with a Turkish rug in the entrance, a blaze of crimson and blue that I carefully avoided with my muddy boots. However, the sight of my patient put all else from my mind.

Gabrielle Danton had once been pretty. I saw that from the fine bone structure of a face that was now almost skeletal and marred by suffering. But death had his hand on her, and would claim her within hours. I administered the cordial and waited until I'd seen her slip into the comforting sleep of the opiate, then left. I could do nothing more for her.

It was some time later that I realized what my reconciliation with Armand would mean to my subversive activities. Believing that I no longer wished to avoid him, he would cease to leave prior word of his intention to visit the Conciergerie, which once again put my system of smuggling in jeopardy. I could have jumped up and down with frustration. Instead, I had to accept his thanks for helping Gabrielle Danton and keep my feelings well hidden until within the privacy of my room. There I kicked my trunk, bruised my toes and shed a few tears of pain, before setting to work to devise another scheme.

I began to cross paths with Armand on a fairly regular basis, as he gave much of his time and surgical skill to the inhabitants of the poorer sections, and I sometimes drank a glass of wine with him after the day's work was over. The contrast with Peter was considerable, and I was confused over whether I really liked the man. He could be quite abrasive at times, yet I enjoyed his company.

We had already found many interests in common during our first meeting. These interests went beyond medicine, to music – he'd heard Mozart play in Vienna – and literature – we argued amicably over Rousseau's avant-garde ideas. We did not, by unspoken agreement, mention politics. Nor did he ever question me about my original methods of people smuggling. That episode had been expunged.

I discovered a deep-seated vein of humour in his nature that invested our conversations with wit and laughter. He was a stimulating conversationalist, failing to bore me, as Peter did, with descriptions of English country society or lists of the advantages of a safe life across the Pas de Calais. No, all Armand did was unwittingly to prevent me from arranging any rescues!

One day he arrived at Mère Poisson's door with two saddle horses and invited me to ride with him in the Bois. I was sorely tempted. Surely, I could take a morning away from my work. It had been so long....

Armand cupped his hands invitingly, and I surrendered to temptation. I flew up into the saddle and spent the next few minutes gaining control of a spirited little mare. The following two hours spent amongst trees and glades in the company of another rider who liked to extend his mount were amongst the happiest since my father died. The wind in my face seemed to blow away the cobwebby mantle of care that had settled over me since I entered the grey stone precincts of the Conciergerie. Now the air tasted differently, my lungs filled to capacity, blood rushed to my cheeks. When we finally halted, I was breathless, exhilarated and grateful, and in no state to refuse Armand's carefully worded request for me to put aside my prejudices and agree to meet with George Danton.

'He is so grateful to you for easing Gabrielle's last hours. The poor devil was half crazed with grief to know that she had died without him being there. Now he has recovered and wishes to express his deep appreciation.'

'There is no need,' I began, feeling queasy at the thought of being in the same room as Danton, one of the architects of Revolution.

''Twould be wise, and useful to you, as well. The support of such an important figure could be beneficial, should you ever need it.' His tone was significant. I felt that he was not threatening, but warning that there might come a time in the future when I needed such support.

'There is something in what you say.' Once again I was called upon to be pragmatic, to put aside my disillusionment with the regime for possible future good.

'Then, shall we say eight o'clock on the next tenth-day holiday at the Café du Foy?'

So, all too soon, and in some trepidation, I joined the great man and Armand in sipping the distilled stars created by Remy Moët, and watching the passing crowd of prosperous Parisians bent on an evening's entertainment in the courtyard of the Palais Royal. The Café du Foy, brilliant with gas lamps and mirrors and the gaiety of well-fed, well-wined patrons, was only one of many to be found within this four-storey quadrangle surrounded by arcades. With almost two hundred shops at its perimeters, the basements and upper storeys featured scores of gambling clubs and some of the city's most notorious brothels. There were many other *places* in this area of the wealthy where one could stroll and take the air beneath avenues of trees, or dance to the music of fine orchestras. But there was none more popular than the Palais Royal. It was the glittering centre of Paris, once the tourist centre of all Europe.

George Danton did not fit his surroundings. He was a huge bull of a man in his early thirties, with a scarred and misshapen face that would have repulsed had he not exuded a force that irradiated all who stood nearby. A gluttonous, power-hungry womanizer, he had the power to fascinate. I sat like a light-mesmerized rabbit listening to him expound upon his favourite topic: the grandeur of the Revolution. He did have the courtesy to thank me beforehand for my services to his wife. However, once having drunk a toast to my health in the first of many glasses of champagne, he embarked on an all too convincing political discourse. I saw the admiration in Armand's face and, most alarming, felt my prejudices being insidiously undermined.

The man was too clever for me.

When I spoke of Marat's outburst at the Cordeliers and his blood lust, Danton deplored this, vehemently, citing his own resignation from the club and adding, 'There are many more of us who regard Marat as a liability who will one day be struck down for his crazy ranting.'

'What of the less extreme sector of the Convention, the Girondins?' I queried. 'It seems that the Jacobins and Cordeliers wish to see them brought down.'

'I am opposed to the Girondins, who are too eloquent and

87

dazzling in their patriotism, loving to declaim, achieving little. They are vain and exclusive, too fastidious to strike hands with me and others such as Robespierre, who in many respects shares my aims.'

I ventured to ask, 'What aims are these?'

'A new national system of education, a strong army and a new system of government entirely. The country is in crisis and the Convention wastes time in factional fighting while royalists are gaining in the west.' His voice rose to a roar, his huge fist banging on the table and making the glasses jingle. 'I tell you, a radical Paris is the only force to which the National Convention can look in resisting Austria and the allies to the north-east and the reactionaries in the interior. Paris is the natural and constituted centre of free France. It is the centre of light. When Paris shall perish there will no longer be a republic!'

I let out my held breath, no longer wondering at him holding sway in the Convention with his rhetoric. It was not only his words, but his delivery. The man was afire with a passionate cause and it showed in every fibre. As the evening lengthened I could feel myself being drawn in. I understood the need for revolution. I understood the need for a new way of governing, a strong rule by strong men. Yet, Danton had voted for the king's death. Danton loved money and power and the good things they brought. Could he be trusted? I needed to go away and think, far from his overwhelming personality and persuasive tongue.

The evening ended and, once back in my eyrie, I found that some of the rhetorical magic had worn off. I decided that if Armand's aim had been to win me over to revolutionary fervour, he had failed.

I returned to my preoccupation with finding a new way to save the aristo children while earning the money to help the starvelings. Yet, I just could not think of any method that wasn't

insanely dangerous. I cursed my short-sightedness in recon-
ciling with Armand, while a part of me was glad, a part that had
been missing him without knowing it. If only he were not such
a devoted disciple of the Revolution he'd be the companion of
my choice: intelligent, kind, professionally interesting, willing
to debate any subject, most particularly his unfortunate political
stance. I usually managed to avoid the latter.

He was even, by now, comfortable with my dual way of life.
He gave me respect, while not hesitating to point out any defi-
ciencies in my medical experience. In turn, he accepted the
things I could teach him. My father had been innovative, and
I'd continued to experiment with drugs and procedures which
sometimes turned out to be of great benefit to the sick. Armand,
as skilled and important as any in his field, was not too proud
to learn from others.

I really tried to arrive at a solution for my problem. I lay
awake at night devising schemes, each more elaborate and
impossible than the one before. Nothing useful occurred to me.
Meanwhile children died and, the source of extra money having
dried up, the people I'd been helping were forced to battle alone
with the grinding poverty and increasing food shortages. I
seemed to feel the reproachful sunken gaze of the street waifs
piercing me as I passed, and I imagined their feeling of aban-
donment.

By March the war was going badly, so badly that the
Convention, already facing a ferocious civil war in the Vendée
against tens of thousands of peasants, voted to establish a
Committee of Public Safety with far-reaching powers. I was not
the only one to fear that all moderation was stifled. Danton,
previously the voice of reason, was attacking the Girondins, and
mad Marat was heading the most extreme of the *sans-culottes*
in marches against the more moderate elements of the
Convention.

It was during these days of unrest that I answered a knock at my door and Camille fell into my arms, laughing and crying with joy.

With the first excitement over, I was full of questions. 'What are you doing in Paris? How did you find me? Where are you staying? Is it safe for you as an aristo? How is little Jean-Claude?'

Camille, who was looking old and tired, still had the same beautiful smile. Beneath her tight-fitting coat she was dressed as a bourgeoise in simple skirt and bodice with fichu, and instead of feathers, she wore the tricolour cockade in her hat.

She said, 'My husband, Claude, is a deputy in the National Convention. I followed him to Paris as soon as Jean-Claude, who is very well and already walking, could travel. We lead a quiet life and are safe enough, although Claude, as a moderate, is concerned over the future.'

I, too, had reservations. However, I kept them to myself, saying, facetiously, 'And finding me? Has my fame spread to the mansions of the Faubourg Saint-Honoré?'

'In a way. I know Peter Lombard. He attends the small salon we patronize in the home of Madame Theresia Renault. When he mentioned the work of a certain Doctor Roussel amongst the poor of Faubourg Saint-Antoine, I knew it must be you.'

'A salon! In these times.'

'I know. We must have some occupation for our minds – some of us more than others,' she added, with a laugh. 'I'm no great intellect, but 'tis an excuse to exchange mild gossip and forget the reality outside the walls of our homes.'

'And who can blame you.' All the same, I sensed the worry beneath my friend's gay manner.

'You must visit us and renew acquaintance with your godson.'

I gaped at her. 'My godson?'

'You took your vows in absentia. You do not object?'

I blinked back a sudden tear. 'I'm so honoured, Camille. My little godson. The first child I delivered.'

'Who would not have lived, save for your skill, my dear. Now, I must hear all about you and your work, and we shall make an arrangement for you to attend the salon to meet some of my friends.'

'And Jean-Claude, as well?'

'Of course.'

We spent a happy hour together before Camille had to leave. I promised to call in the Rue Saint-Denis very soon and, at her insistence, in the genuine persona of her friend, Juliette Roussel. It would be a rare opportunity to enjoy relief from care.

I found Theresia Renault's little salon to be an extraordinary experience, as though I'd stepped through a doorway into an artificial world where men and women talked about matters that had no connection with reality. Well, not with my reality of prisons and sickness and poverty.

Here, in the elegantly gilded and plastered rooms there was candlelight and perfume and the chink of delicate china cups. Mirrored walls reflected a kaleidoscope of rainbow silks, jewels and faces powdered and patched beyond recognition. Conversation was elegant and witty, sometimes intellectual, always light as a dandelion puff. Nothing serious, nothing to do with the outside world was permitted to intrude. This was a place where values did not matter, but appearances did; where the sting of satire was applied delicately; where esoteric subjects chosen with care were picked apart, artfully woven into new patterns and gracefully laid to rest. It was clever. It entertained. It was an anodyne for people too terrified to leave their counterfeit reality, since the old one had been destroyed.

My reservations did not prevent my enjoying certain aspects

of this peculiar society. I loved the poetry readings and the occasional battle of wits between the more learned members. And there was music, such as I'd never heard. I could have listened to the young violinist for ever. However, the falseness of the whole thing soon grated on my nerves, and had it not been for two special people, I'd have ceased to visit the house in Rue Faubourg Saint-Honoré.

I could see that Camille needed the pretence. She attended in full dress, powered and rouged. Surrounded by her own kind, she could believe in the maintenance of her aristocratic status, although she'd actually sunk to the level of a bourgeoise, keeping house for her equally disenfranchised husband and her little boy.

Jean-Claude was a delight. She brought him with her especially for my sake and, when the affected atmosphere of the salon became too much for me, I could steal away and play with this almost one-year-old cherub. All children are dear to me but, as the first child I'd ever delivered, and my godson, he had a special place in my heart. I thanked the deity in whom I had no real belief that he'd escaped the fate of the babes in the Conciergerie.

And that thought increased my guilt at having failed to renew my smuggling activities. Over the summer, in my own district of Saint-Antoine, a full half score infants had been struck down by a terrible inflammation of the bowels, caused, I had no doubt, by the fetid water they drank. Only the rich could afford to have barrels of fresh spring water brought in until heavy rains swept the streets and refilled the sunken wells. Here I'd been wasting time when children were dying. I really *had* to find a new method.

CHAPTER 9

P ETER CONTINUED TO be my faithful follower, no matter how
I tried to dissuade him. His demonstrations of affection
stayed within the bounds of those permitted to a friend, but he
had developed a most irritating habit. He became increasingly
critical of the situation in Paris and beyond. From the vantage
point of an onlooker he favoured me unceasingly with his opinions of the government, the mob and the conduct of the war, to
the point where I actually taxed him with voyeurism. It wasn't
very fair of me, I knew. Why should I expect a foreigner to
understand French affairs? I think I was just so concerned over
the increased level of brutality, as the Committee of Public
Safety delivered ever more victims to the executioner, and fear
hung over Paris like an invisible pall.

Stupidly, one evening when we dined out I told Peter he
should cease carping and either go home to England or help do
something about the horrific waste of life in my country. Too
late, I knew I'd revealed myself, and he wasn't slow to understand.

He leaned across the table and said softly, 'You are involved
in some kind of clandestine activity. I might have guessed.
You have such a generous spirit, of course you would be unable
to stand by and do nothing. No wonder you despise me
for staying aloof.' He'd gone pale, and the stiffening of his

shoulders warned me that he was about to make a great effort. 'Tell me, Juliette. How can I help?'

I'd goaded him into an unacceptable position, and I was ashamed. I said more warmly, 'I should not have accused you, Peter, and I ask forgiveness. I do appreciate your kind offer. However, 'tis not your affair.'

'No. But your involvement makes it so.'

I felt very badly indeed. Touching his hand, fleetingly, I said, 'Peter, I cannot take advantage of … of your fondness for me. You should go home before you are swept up in the carnage.'

His smile twisted a little. 'My dear, you take no advantage. We have a saying in England: "Hobson's Choice", which is to say, no choice at all. Do you think I could leave now, knowing the dangers you face?'

I'd lost one battle and won another. There was no doubt of Peter's usefulness in my proposed scheme, and I knew that I would use him. The lives of the children still came first.

My new plan was simple, and would probably only work once, yet it was better than doing nothing at all. Nor was it likely that Armand would discover it, even if we crossed paths at the crucial time. I chose two young boys of a suitable age and size and worked with them, accustoming them to being mesmerized, then waited like a ghoul for someone to die.

Using his own money, for mine had gone, Peter hired a horse and cart to be ready when required. He also practised changing his appearance. In shirt and sabots, hair straggling from beneath the red cap, he made a creditable ruffian. His terrible French would be a difficulty, but if he were approached he'd just have to play dumb and surly.

On the day that a frail elderly prisoner died of fluid on the lungs, we were ready.

Poor Citoyen Mercier's body was treated to a cosmetic change to give the appearance of plague, with painted pustules and, as an added touch, a good drenching with valerian and certain other vile-smelling herbs guaranteed to ward off any inquisitiveness. It was then placed in the specially constructed coffin I had brought in. Beneath its false floor lay the two children, squeezed tightly end-to-end. The air holes were inconspicuous, and they slept peacefully in their tranquil world. Most importantly, the dead man had weighed little more than a child, and since no one wished for more than a brief glance at the horrid-looking face revealed for inspection beneath an almost closed lid, I believed the plan would work.

This didn't stop my heart from thundering like a runaway team as we approached the clerk's desk. I'd waited until it was almost time for the changing of the guard, when the men would be eager to be off, and the clerk was ready to close his book and think about his dinner. The carriers, ignorant of the trick, helped us by evincing a strong distaste for their job. They wore cloth steeped in vinegar across their lower faces, and thick gloves, as well as the expression of men anxious to drop their load and run.

And so it happened just as I'd hoped. Everyone backed away from the box as it was carried out and loaded on to Peter's waiting cart. No one seemed pleased by my tainted company, either. I set off on foot for Camille's residence in the Rue Saint-Denis and my rendezvous with Peter and his charges. What arrangements he'd made for the corpse, he kept to himself. It was my job to waken the children and have them cared for by Camille until the *clandestines* called.

I felt I'd wronged Camille, thinking her flighty and unable to cope with reality, when in fact she agreed instantly to my tentative proposal that she take in the children. I arrived to find them tucked up in bed, still peacefully sleeping, and Camille watching by their side.

Her lovely blue eyes glinted with moisture as she turned to

me, saying, 'They are little more than babes. How could anyone wish to kill them?'

I'd asked myself the same question too often. 'I do not believe the men who sign the documents give any thought to the lives they cut off. 'Tis simply their daily work, ridding their country of troublemakers.'

'Oh, Juliette, what has our country come to, with children murdered in the name of liberty?'

I had no answer.

The following day I reported to the prison authorities that the rumour of plague had been false. Apparently the unfortunate Citoyen Mercier had suffered from a combination of diseases that counterfeited the one most dreaded, and I apologized for any inconvenience caused by the scare. I was made to feel that my reputation as a physician had suffered a blow, and held my head low for a time.

It was harder to maintain an air of innocence when Armand later questioned me over the mistaken diagnosis. However, whether or not it could be called a fortunate instance, the uproar caused by Marat and his cohorts' success in overthrowing the Girondins certainly turned Armand's thoughts in another direction.

It had become a habit for him to call upon me to assist with more than ordinarily difficult surgical operations. I found this interesting, adding to my store of knowledge, and I was proud to be considered a competent honorary *sous chirurgien*. One afternoon we'd left such a patient in the Rue Saint-Honoré and were walking down towards the Tuileries when the sound of the mob reached us. We raced towards the entrance to find ourselves on the perimeter of a vast crowd. Thousands of demonstrators, along with the National Guard, were besieging the Convention and demanding the arrest of members of the Girondin party.

Armand was jubilant. 'At last we are rid of those pro-royalists with their vacillation and fine phrases full of air. Now we shall see proper government and proper prosecution of the war.'

Normally I'd have fired up immediately in protest. Today I found myself agreeing that something drastic must be done before France was overrun by her enemies. It was confusing. He could be so annoying and wrong, yet here I was in part agreement with him. My true sympathies, of course, were with the men who had been trying to keep a balance in government, to keep at bay the extremists who knew no law but their own will. And I feared very much for Camille, whose husband was a moderate supporting the Girondins.

'What will happen to them?' I asked.

He shrugged. 'They will probably be placed under house arrest until being brought to trial.'

I felt the blood leave my cheeks, and stumbled before catching myself up. Everyone knew the short step from arrest to the guillotine, including family members. Camille! Little Jean-Claude!

Armand put out a hand to steady me. 'What is it? Why do you look like that?'

''Tis nothing. A momentary spasm.'

'What kind of spasm? Where?'

I made myself smile. 'There is no need for you to fall into medical mode, my friend. I am well enough.' Despite my anxiety I noted the ease with which I'd claimed friendship with him. When had that happened? How could it? How could I feel this strange new warmth towards a man whose political beliefs were a betrayal of his very calling?

He was watching me closely. 'You are not to be trusted,' he said. 'You are too tender-hearted. Let someone in need cross your path and you plunge in to help, regardless of law, of danger, of right or wrong.'

I summoned cool reason to my aid, pointing to the mob still milling around and cheering one another. 'I had rather be foolishly sensitive than celebrate the impending destruction of good men who tried to serve their country.'

My criticism made him curt. 'They could have been more accommodating and retained their positions. Danton tried to make them allies, but they would not listen. The warning was there months ago. They were deliberately blind to the danger, as well as deaf.'

'They did what they thought was best, perhaps not wisely or well, yet they don't deserve to die for it.' Now I had a genuine pain in my head. I was wasting time arguing. I needed to see Camille, to make sure of her safety.

I was never very good at hiding my emotions.

Armand's voice softened and the tension between us melted away as he said, 'Once again we fall into the trap of political argument. We should simply agree to disagree, since you have proved that not even Danton can change your attitude. Yet I would be a friend to you. And as a friend I must warn you not to become involved in this latest upset. If you have Girondist connections, be wary how you approach them lest you be tainted by proximity. I doubt if any members remaining in Paris after today can be saved.' He walked away, leaving me to wonder if he was a mind reader.

Of course, I ignored his warning and went to Camille's house. Although I made my approach circumspectly, I need not have bothered. The door was barred and guarded, the curtains drawn at the windows. People passed by on the other side of the street, eyes averted, while others, obvious *sans culottes*, stood and jeered, foretelling a trip to the guillotine.

I went home, sick at heart and wondering what next would fall upon this beleaguered city.

I was soon to know. In mid July a young woman, a Girondist

supporter, travelled to Paris with murder on her mind, and mad Marat met his well-deserved fate. Charlotte Corday had the courage – or was it insanity? – to martyr herself by stabbing the monster in his bath, the place where he regularly worked and conducted business while trying to ease the itching of his diseased body. His followers, on hearing the news, would have torn her apart had she not been hustled away to prison. Foiled, they rose *en masse* and Paris rioted.

CHAPTER 10

I WALKED RIGHT into the storm. I've been told that I must have been blind and deaf not to have realized what was happening. Possibly I was. Absorbed in my worries over Camille, who was still under house arrest, as far as I knew, and concerned over a wave of gastric illness sweeping through my district and killing so many of the weak, I had no notion that I was heading straight into a mighty upsurge of grief and fury over the killing of a man I considered a monster.

To many of the lower classes Marat was a beloved figure. He was a fighter for their cause, whose brutal attacks in his journal and every other public arena were as music to the down-trodden. As word of his death was carried through the streets of every section, people came together howling for revenge against someone, anyone. Charlotte Corday was beyond their reach but there were other scapegoats. Anybody who had ever said a word against the Revolution would do. Anybody who even looked as though he might say such a word was meat to their ravening appetite for reprisal.

All this I learned later. At the time I was only vaguely aware of noise in the distance, growing louder as I went on my round of bedridden patients. The day was one of summer's best, of cloudless skies and a cleansing breeze blowing through the narrow streets, carrying away some of the worst odours. A storm on the previous evening had helped to empty the kennels and there were even a few window boxes displaying blooms. My mind drifted to past summers when I'd ridden out with my father on similar errands, but through fields of crops, past hedges thick with berries and animals standing hock deep in grass – an apparently contented countryside somnolent under the hot sun.

By the time I'd been jerked back to the present by the increasing uproar, I'd turned a corner, and there they were, wild-eyed men and women in their striped trousers and red caps, marching and shouting and waving all manner of weapons, from broomsticks to swords. And in their midst were knots of disturbance growing bigger by the minute as some unfortunate was turned upon, seized and beaten to the ground before being strung up on a lamp post, or simply had his throat cut.

Before my eyes a man with his clothes torn to shreds was being dragged along by the ankles, his head dissolving into a bloodied mass as it beat against the cobbles. A woman's shriek rose above the roar of the mob, and I saw others trampled beneath an army of boots and clogs. People fled by me like rabbits before a pack of hunting dogs and, too late, I turned to join them.

Rough hands grabbed my collar and a dirty face leered into mine, mouthing something unintelligible. My nostrils filled with the odour of killing fever, a compound of drink and sweat and an unnameable animal stink that I momentarily associated with slavering jaws. More hands grasped my arms, tearing my coat in two as I pulled away. My feet slipped, I stumbled and I lost my medical bag.

'Here's one,' screeched a woman. Her eyes were as feral as a cat's as she sprang at me, tearing off my neckcloth and stuffing it in her bosom. 'Look at his pretty face. See his dainty linen. A filthy aristo-lover. Cut him up, boys. Let's see him bleed like our brave, holy Marat.'

I'd never been so afraid. Fear has a flavour, a metallic taste upon the tongue, its odour reaching up into the nostrils and wreathing itself about the brain. It strangles thought while it galvanizes the nerves and muscles. I struggled desperately, wrenching against my captors, deafened by the shouting and screaming, my own voice drowned as I babbled that I was a doctor, a patriot. Someone spat in my face. My hair was yanked painfully as I fell and was dragged and kicked amongst a forest of legs. With my hands wound protectively about my head, I saw the murderous woman lunge, knife in hand, and thought my time had come.

Then suddenly I was on my feet, encircled by a strong arm and dragged back against a set of steps.

A raucous female voice sounded above my head, 'Hé, mes amis. This isn't your meat. This is the good doctor who tends your children without payment.' She broke off and delivered a well-aimed kick at the crotch of an attacker who was clearly not listening to her. Dropping his stave, he fell backwards with a curse, clutching at his genitals. Men nearby laughed. So did the woman holding me upright.

'Onwards, patriot soldiers!' she cried. 'There's work for you yet in seeking out the traitorous dogs who would kill the Revolution. Onwards! In the name of our great Marat. And sing, that they may hear you coming and shit their pants with fear.'

There was a great roar of approval, and moments later the sound of the 'Marseillaise' rose to drown out the cries of victims as the rioters moved on to spread a terror that would end only with the elaborate obsequies for their beloved Marat.

I didn't move a muscle until the mob had gone by. Nor did my saviour, until, with the passing of the last group, she released her iron clutch on my ribs and let me slide down into a sitting position against the steps. Arms akimbo, she stood looking down at me, her expression scarcely reassuring.

Looking back at her I saw a young Amazon, a typical *poissard* of the fish markets, whose brawny forearms displayed the strength of a man, even though they issued from a low-necked bodice giving every evidence of the female sex. The woman's skirt was kilted up to show a ragged, striped underskirt and stockings with holes, and on her greasy curls she wore the red cap of liberty.

Feeling very much like one of her fish, freshly landed, I gasped, 'A thousand thanks, *citoyenne*. I thought I was spent.'

'So you should be,' she said harshly. 'Only a fool stays on the street when the *enragés* march.'

'I didn't know. That is … I heard Marat's name—' I trailed off. Hatred emanated from her, like a blast of heat.

'Aye. They did for him. Some woman was their tool, but those *sacré* Girondist pigs got him. May their guts rot in the fires of Hell!' Her ferocity died slowly, to be followed by a grin that grew wider as she surveyed my dishevelment. '*Merde*! You're a woman!'

I looked down to see my shirt torn from my shoulders and one pink-tipped breast very much in evidence. Well, denial was obviously useless, and I had no energy to spend on equivocation, let alone an attempt to flee. 'Yes. I'm a woman, doing a man's job in a world that labels me inferior.'

One of those brawny arms descended and I got a clap on the shoulder that almost flattened me.

'*Citoyenne*, I salute you. You're one of us, for all your fancy clothes and fine ways. Is not this Revolution for women, too? Do we not march and fight in the street, side by side with our brothers? The day is coming when we'll have the equality we deserve.' She peered more closely at my face, then hauled me upright. 'Come. I'll see you safe at your lodgings. Stay off the streets until this is over, you understand?'

I was all but lifted off my feet and half-carried back to Rue Bitone where I was relinquished into the arms of a clucking Mère Poisson. She looked disapprovingly at my rescuer, but was too busy exclaiming over my hurts and mourning the loss of my so-called 'fancy' coat to express her doubts. I managed to learn the name of Maxine LeBrun and her address before she left and I submitted to my landlady's ministrations. This was the second time I'd been brought home in a distressed state, and it embarrassed me. I really had to stop walking with my mind in another sphere and pay attention to my surroundings. Paris was a dangerous city, and becoming more so each day.

My first step in this direction two days later was to the flea market to purchase a not-too-used coat in the approved blue of the tricolour. With my mended white shirt and a slightly battered hat sporting a cockade, I was the *patriot de jour*, and could, I hoped, negotiate the streets in safety. I bemoaned the fate of my medical equipment, some of which was irreplaceable, but secured whatever I could in the way of knives and bandages, the latter being of fine weave and torn from the habits of nuns who no longer needed them.

My next step was a visit to Maxine Lebrun. I not only wished to express my thanks more fully, but to ensure that my dual lifestyle remained a secret. Word spread through the local intelligence service like chain lightning.

I found her at the fish market in Les Halles, attempting to rally a group of her co-workers for a march on a suspected food-hoarding merchant. She was a rousing speaker, yet I could see her audience today was apathetic, possibly too tired from their exertions of the previous day, which had marked the interment of Marat.

With a snort of disgust, Maxine climbed down from her

perch, a pile of crates smelling strongly of fish, and greeted me with, 'They want to see the Corday woman lose her head today. I've seen so many, what's one more – even a murderess.'

'I thought you'd be glad to see her suffer for her crime,' I remarked, curious to understand the way this Valkyrie thought. She'd seemed so full of hatred when I first met her.

She shrugged. ''Tis over with. She'll pay the price, like all the other treacherous bourgeois who would destroy us, but 'twill not bring Marat back.'

While her features were quite coarse, she had the loveliest dark eyes. Now these filmed over and, astonishingly, a tear fell. 'His funeral was so beautiful,' she said, leading me out into the street where the smell of rotting fish was, thankfully, not so strong. 'All the people fell to their knees as he passed in his burial car drawn by young girls dressed in white, carrying wands and branches of cypress, and followed by the whole of the Convention and municipal authorities. The Sections marched beneath their banners singing patriotic hymns, and the people kneeling and watching sobbed and chanted a prayer: "Oh heart of Jesus! Oh sacred heart of Marat!" And they placed his heart in a porphyry urn and suspended it from the ceiling of the Cordeliers' Club where all may see it and worship.'

I swallowed my discomfort at such blasphemy – particularly surprising in view of Marat's militant atheism – and made some sort of approving sound.

Maxine blew her nose in her fingers and recovered her poise. She remarked that it was a pity I'd missed such a sight and took me home to supper.

She had an arrangement with the local baker who exchanged his goods for certain unspecified services, and his rolls were delicious. But the cheese was maggoty and the poor excuse for a soup was the most meagre I'd yet encountered. Maxine clearly lived her creed of share and share alike and down with the food hoarders.

Her poverty was obvious from the sparsity of her room adjoining a public laundry which created a constant damp atmosphere reeking of soda and sweaty garments. But her life was spent on the streets haranguing everyone she met on the need to preserve the Revolution. She was driven, totally given over to her vision of the New France.

I could sympathize, despite her dangerous fanaticism. For the first time in her deprived life, opportunity was there for her and all the rest of the country's underprivileged caste to have a say in their future. I understood, but I was anxious. Maxine and Marat and others like them had no sense of boundaries. Like children, they grasped at what they wanted without seeing where such need or greed would lead. There was only black and white in their world – *sacré* aristos versus the people, the privileged versus the downtrodden.

'I'm a *vainqueur de la Bastille*, you know,' she said through a mouthful of bread and cheese. Her teeth were the blackened stumps of so many of the poor, and even if she'd had meat I doubt if she could have eaten it.

'You actually took part in the charge?' I didn't know whether to be impressed or appalled.

Her dark eyes flashed as she looked right through me, remembering. 'They shot him. It was just a peaceful demonstration and the dragoons opened fire without any warning.'

'What?' The reports I had of that day were entirely different. However, Maxine looked back to an earlier event, and I could not mistake the rage and pain accompanying that memory.

'My man, my Giraud. We were to be wed. But he joined a deputation asking for fairer taxes, and they shot him. He died in my arms. I swore on that day to avenge him.'

'And so you joined in the attack on the Bastille.' Now I knew what drove her. Grief, patriotism and the desire for vengeance were a potent mix. No wonder she spent her days inciting citizens against the partisans of tyranny.

I shifted on my packing-case seat and added, 'I suppose you were one of the women who marched on Versailles three months later?'

'Aye, and took part in the storming of the Tuileries, and the bread riots. There are many of us women taking the law into our own hands. You should join us.'

That took me by surprise. Of course, her evangelical fervour should have warned me. Once again I'd failed to see danger ahead.

Gathering my wits, I said, 'Nothing would please me more. However, my work is too important for me to leave. I save lives every day, Maxine, lives of the poor and disadvantaged, children who will soon be ready to join in the fight to save France from her enemies. We need every soldier. We need healthy men working in the armaments factories.'

'You save the lives of *sacré* aristos!' she spat. Rearing up against the table and setting the soup pot slopping.

I shot to my feet, knowing that the only way to deal with her was to be equally resolute. I leaned across the board and spoke sternly. 'Yes, I save them for a brief time before they're claimed by Madame Guillotine. And do you know why? Because I must eat. Because I must stay alive if I'm to help the Revolution.' I met her fierce gaze and returned it.

Suddenly she laughed and slapped me again on the shoulder, the same one she'd bruised before, and sent me staggering. '*Hé*, I like you, little *docteur*. You talk sense. And you do very well in a man's world. You show them what a woman can do, eh?'

'Only if my secret is preserved,' I pointed out. 'Promise not to reveal it, Maxine, or my value will be lost. I need my job in the Conciergerie.'

'Aye. 'Tis safe with me. And if any give you trouble, send for me.'

I didn't need her suddenly grim expression to underline the offer. Lord alone knew what tribes of ferocious women were at her command. I sincerely hoped that I'd never have cause to anger this volatile daughter of the Revolution.

CHAPTER 11

C AMILLE WAS MUCH in my thoughts and I desperately needed to know that she was not in any kind of need. Outright bribery had its dangers. The guard on the house in Rue Saint-Denis changed regularly, and there were bound to be fanatical patriots amongst them who wouldn't hesitate to denounce me. I decided on boldness, instead.

The family must eat, so I disguised myself as a delivery boy, packed a basket with suitable viands, and presented myself at the door of Camille's house. The fact that a bottle of wine fell into the hands of the current guard was neither here nor there. That was simple courtesy, not a bribe. The risk was small and well worth the greeting I received.

Once inside the door, I was hailed by Camille with delight.

'My dearest Juliette! How wonderful!'

She held me tightly, then stepped back and began to laugh. 'How ridiculous you look in your cap and apron! So much the urchin. Where did you find such terrible trousers?'

I was happy to amuse her. Clearly there'd been little to laugh about in the weeks of her incarceration. Her normal bloom had faded and she'd lost weight. She also had a persistent slight cough that worried me. I said, 'The trousers are Jaseur's best, I'll have you know, and only loaned to me upon the strict under-standing that they are returned in good order.'

'How is Jaseur … and good Mère Poisson?' Camille drew me down on to an elegant chaise that was gritty with dust. The whole room had an unkempt appearance. Candlewax marred a lovely inlaid table top and glass and mirrors were smeared. No servants, I supposed, and a mistress who had no idea how to clean house.

I answered her questions as well as I could, but not to her satisfaction, since these were mainly concerned with her friends and their activities. I reflected that she seemed to have little interest in current events. This could have been deliberate, on the lines of 'what we don't know will not affect us'. Camille had always tended to hide from unpleasantness. I was torn between wanting to keep her advised of the political situation and feeling that she'd rather not think about the future. There was no question of my being able to help her escape. There were plenty of antagonistic eyes watching the houses of the Girondist families, quite apart from official guards.

Camille's husband did not appear, and she excused this as his 'occupation with affairs' in his book room. I could well believe that he'd rather not meet me in my present guise. Despite his Republican leanings, he was an aristocrat to his polished finger-tips, and would not find me congenial. As for news of the world outside, he'd have his ways of obtaining this.

I was more than content to spend the few minutes that I could spare with little Jean-Claude. He seemed healthy enough, although I wished he could exercise his legs running in the park in fresh air. He didn't remember me, which made me sad, but he was happy to play with anyone who offered. I could have spent an hour with him. Instead, after five minutes I said to Camille, 'I must not stay any longer or my impersonation of a delivery boy will collapse. I will try to find another way to see you, but it may not be easy.'

She clung to me, and I saw the fear in her eyes as I tore myself away and left with my empty basket on my arm. When would I see her again, and under what circumstances?

Marat's death had brought a frightening fresh impetus to the Revolution. In the weeks that followed, on several occasions I overheard former strong adherents questioning the direction in which they were being swept at an ever-increasing pace. And most worrying of all was the behaviour of the Extremists under the new head of the Committee of Public Safety.

This was made clear to me some days after my visit to Camille. I'd left Maxine's room, carrying my medical bag which she'd somehow saved for me, when I collided with Armand, who was hurrying from the laundry next door. We both dived at the same time to catch his parcel of fresh linen, banging heads. My eyes watered as I stepped aside with an apology.

'Not at all. 'Twas my error.' He seemed unusually distracted.

I pointed out that his parcel was beginning to slip from beneath his arm. To retrieve it he dropped his bag, which flew open to reveal, not just the instruments of his profession, but a bundle of poppets made from odd pieces of wood, with painted faces and bits of ragged skirt attached. Gifts for his small patients, I surmised, and hid a smile. Who was he to accuse me of tender-heartedness?

He said ruefully as he gathered his goods, 'As you see, my mind is not in the same place as my body.' Then frowning, he added, 'Walk with me, I pray you.'

Intrigued by this unusual behaviour, I joined him and waited to hear what he had to say.

At first he was silent. We'd covered half the distance back to the river before he began with a question. 'Have you heard that George Danton lost his position heading the Committee of Public Safety?'

'I had heard that Citoyen Robespierre took his place,' I answered cautiously. Danton's fall from grace had been a talking point amongst the people of my neighbourhood. Not everyone had supported his milder tactics in the months when he'd negotiated with 'enemy' countries. I'd also heard that the great man had willingly stepped down in order to holiday back at his property in Arcis, along with his new young wife.

Armand scowled. 'Robespierre is dangerous. He and his fellow Extremists have taken over the Cordeliers, and in his absence they denounce Danton from the rostrum for weakness and "lack of revolutionary ardour". They're virtually running the Committee of Public Safety to suit themselves, while George sits back and lets them.'

'Perhaps he needs a rest from political battles,' I suggested. 'He's newly wed, and deserves some time with his family.' I'd been shocked that he could so soon forget his adored Gabrielle. Perhaps he had needed a mother for his children.

''Tis the wrong time to rest.' Armand's frown deepened. 'Twelve fanatics now occupy the former royal private office in the Tuileries. They have a tight hold on centralized power, and I fear they will not be dispensing justice. Robespierre is the most fanatical of them all. He talks of "the poor" as if they are apart from the rest of us, virtuous because of their lack of wealth. He lumps together in one mass the depraved with the decent, the dishonest with the honourable, and he'll use them to alter the course of the Revolution.' His face reddened as he grew more agitated. Now he stopped in the middle of the street and, as if driven beyond caution, shouted, 'God damn him! He's baying for blood, and George and the Girondins and all the rest of the moderates can't see it. If they don't get up off their rumps and do something quickly, they will find themselves marching in step to the guillotine!'

He realized that his outburst had attracted attention, and moderated his tone, but his anger and distress affected me as I listened to his dire prediction. I felt I was seeing a new Armand, his former zeal for the Revolution clouded by disappointment and concern for the outcome.

I, too, was concerned. George Danton might be an opportunist, but he was also shrewd and visionary, and he understood what drove others. If he had semi-retired from the revolutionary battle, then his place could be filled by lesser men whose self-interest could be very damaging. This was already evident in the increasing boldness of the *enragés*, such as Maxine. I said as much, and Armand seized upon my words.

'I agree, and it surprises me to find you here in this cradle of malcontents. You are unwise to make a companion of someone like Maxine Lebrun.'

Once I would have fired up at his criticism. Today I felt it might be warranted. I realized that I'd been growing more and more worried about the way the Revolution was headed, and about the welfare of ordinary folk, such as myself. While I was grateful to Maxine, I could see her becoming more rabid by the day, holding up people in the street and haranguing them, accusing the better dressed of anti-revolutionary tendencies, demanding proof of devotion to the State. She and others like her were embarrassing and, as their numbers increased, were getting beyond control.

Yet I had an obligation. I said, 'I owe Maxine my life. When I was attacked, she plucked me out of a mob crazed by Marat's death.' I waited for his reaction, another rendition of the familiar theme: head in the clouds, lack of common sense, etc. etc.

He threw up his hands, but forbore to comment, which surprised me. So I continued, 'I'm in her debt. Naturally I will respond when she asks for my help.'

'What sort of help? Patching up her rabble band when they've been out on a rampage? I've seen the sort of thing they do to citizens who have earned their distrust.' In a changed voice he said, 'Let me take your place. Citoyenne Lebrun knows she can trust me.'

I hardly knew how to answer. He was mistaken, of course. I felt no such obligation, and had come to patch up Maxine alone, following an accident with her fish-gutting knife which almost lost her a hand. Yet Armand's offer was astonishing. Why this sudden concern for my safety? Was it … could he possibly care for me as more than a friend? My heart seemed to bound at the thought. It seemed as if a sudden bright light had been shed upon my understanding of our relationship, and whether or not I'd misread his feelings, my own were unmistakeable.

My new viewpoint was something of a shock. I'd never known love as it is described by the poets. My mother died when I was very young, and any softness in my father's nature was reserved for the sick. Philippe, my much older brother, had always been reclusive and he left our home for the seminary at an early age. There was Camille, with her affectionate friend-ship, and that was all. Now, with the sudden violence of a summer storm, love, in all its power and wonder was revealed to me.

It was an extraordinary moment. I felt both exalted and exposed, my feelings as naked as a newborn babe. Turning aside, I struggled to hide my confusion. When I eventually faced Armand again, he appeared as normal and controlled as ever. Had I imagined that moment of tenderness? I was afraid so. Yet nothing could quell the spring of gladness inside me, masked by my polite refusal of his offer, but fed by the know-ledge that he cared enough to make it. I was his dear friend, if nothing more. Perhaps, in time, I could *make* it more.

At this inopportune moment I looked down the street and saw Peter Lombard hurrying to meet me. In appearance he was a good deal less the gentleman these days, adapting himself to fit with the working-class area where he now resided, or rather, skulked for safety. However, his attitudes were still all his own.

'I was coming to escort you home,' he said without preamble. 'This is not the sort of district where you should walk alone.'

'Docteur Roussel is not alone, as you see,' responded Armand. His tone was neutral, but I could see Peter bridle, as if he'd been chided.

Poor Peter's jealousy of Armand was so evident. He was caught between wanting to whisk me away and knowing that I would refuse to be taken in charge and protected like a frail female.

He cleared his throat and glared at Armand, who began to look amused.

I'd come to know his unpredictable sense of humour and, fearing that he might bait Peter for entertainment, I said hastily, 'Allow me to present Citoyen Docteur Dumouriez, a colleague.' I turned to Armand. 'M'sieu Lombard is a visitor from England.'

Armand nodded. 'You are taking a risk by remaining in Paris at this time, Englishman.'

Peter said, stiffly, 'I have my reasons.'

'Do they include an interest in the welfare of Citoyenne Juliette Roussel? Come, man. Your whole attitude betrays the frustrated gallant. Clearly you are in the lady's confidence, as am I, although not for any reason that you might suppose.'

Peter's bewildered expression made me want to laugh, even while I could have berated Armand for creating a situation. In no mood for verbal games, I said, 'I have work to do, and I require no escort. I bid you both good day.' And I strode off briskly.

I confess to hiding from Peter in a shabby little market stall behind a mound of onions until I saw him go by. My guilt was outweighed by relief. I simply could not support having to listen to his outpourings all the way back to my lodgings. I needed to think about this overwhelming attraction to Armand, a man who had first been my enemy, then a colleague, then my friend, and who now shone like the most brilliant star in my universe. It was almost too extraordinary to believe.

Looking back, I understood that it had been a matter of stages. This enchantment had grown upon me in tiny increments, like the layering of nacre upon a pearl, each time I met Armand and came to understand him better, each time I heard report of his kindness to the less fortunate. His high reputation amongst the people of the poor sections was a tribute to his selflessness, and the children adored him. In early days I'd thought him callous, because the infant prisoners who caught at my heart seemed not to affect him. I now knew better. He'd simply not allowed himself to care for the ones beyond his help, using his professional detachment as armour against pain. Armand was a good man with, I believed, the capacity to love deeply. The only question was: could he, might he, one day love me?

By midnight I was in an entirely different frame of mind. What did I want with love? There was no place for it in my plans. This was not the time for personal feelings to intrude when my work took all my time and energy, when the whole of France seemed likely to explode into disaster at any minute. What had I been thinking of?

I reminded myself how little I knew about Armand beyond his altruism and professional skill. We shared interests and he had a fine mind that allowed us to match wits, but he never spoke of his background. He had a life before Paris. He might have obligations. He might even be married!

It surprised me how little I cared about any of it.

I tried to be dispassionate. What would it mean to love and be loved – loss or gain? Loss of freedom and independence, or the gaining of strength and support? I didn't want to consider such an equation. Life was difficult enough for us all at present. Why complicate it further?

Back and forth I went in a most exhausting state of indecision, eventually abandoning all hope of sleep.

By breakfast time my weathercock mind had spun itself giddy. Finally I admitted the truth, that something irrevocable had happened to me and I had no option but to accept this inner change. It could, however, be dealt with in private, and with luck it would eventually shrink away and cease to be a torment. I had no illusion that this would be easy.

As for the one moment when I'd thought Armand felt tenderness towards me, it had been a mistake, born of my own shocked realization that I could lose my heart. I'd always been so practical, so sure of my path and my ability to follow it. No one had warned me about paths offering sudden turnings to tempt the traveller into an impasse. My pathway had always been clear, and I was determined that it would remain so, no matter how much I longed to take the delightfully beckoning detour.

That being decided, I set off for the Conciergerie feeling thoroughly out of sorts.

CHAPTER 12

I MADE MY peace with Peter over a meal in Mère Poisson's kitchen as we discussed my latest notion for rescuing a child prisoner. It was more private than a café, and my good landlady could be relied upon to keep a still tongue. Her love for children extended easily to the innocents of all classes, while Jaseur was my constant willing *cavalier servente* and had to be dissuaded from shadowing my footsteps. He acted as messenger between Peter and me, and kept us advised on the informants who appeared like mushrooms in our section from time to time.

The affection was mutual. He was a scamp and constantly in trouble; he was also loyal, thoughtful and had apparently decided that his role in life was to see to my needs. I'd grown increasingly fond of him, and sometimes my thoughts turned to the boy's future, when the Revolution had run its course and, perhaps, there would be avenues for the advancement of the poor. But lately, with conditions deteriorating, I'd grown less sanguine. Peter's definition of the State as a runaway 'heading for Hell at a fast clip' was all too true. And with the recent Law of Suspects coming into force, I was growing increasingly worried about *his* safety.

Prior to laying my new plan before him, I brought up this difficult subject once more.

'Peter, the new Vigilance Committees are very active in the

sections. They traffic in these "good citizenship certificates" for which, as a foreigner, you're not eligible. You could so easily be stopped in the street and arrested.'

He shook his blond head, which he now wore long and shaggy to match his workman's clothes. 'I'm safe enough while I'm careful. I carry false papers, as you know, and I've paid someone to exclude me from the list of suspects.' He sighed, obviously regretting his former lifestyle amongst his peers. However, those days in France were gone.

The salons had closed, the *frequenters* scattered in fear or imprisoned in their homes, as was Camille. Many of the bourgeois who had thought the Revolution didn't concern them were learning, to their cost, that they were not immune. This new law made suspect any citizens who could not give satisfactory account of their means of support or their discharge of civic obligations. And it operated beyond Paris, casting a cold shadow over the whole country, the shadow of the guillotine.

Peter shivered, as if sensing my thoughts. He refused to give way to his growing apprehension, but only a fool or a madman would not be afraid these days.

He said, 'Have you been in contact with the Comte de Cassonnière and his wife?'

'I've seen Camille twice in past weeks, only briefly. The guards have become more suspicious since several escape attempts by certain Girondists. All food must be examined and handed in by the guards. No one else enters. Camille did manage to smuggle out one message, but there's been nothing since then. As far as I know, she and her husband and little Jean-Claude are well enough, although she must fear the future.' The fear would be closer to terror, I knew, despite Camille's effort to appear normal. Being helpless in the matter, I tried not to think about it.

Peter was sensitive enough to leave the subject. 'Tell me about your new scheme for the children of the Conciergerie.'

It was my turn to sigh. 'Nothing so grand, I'm afraid. It's another of those ideas that will probably work only the once. I'm so grateful for your help, Peter. I couldn't do this without you.'

He blushed with pleasure. 'You know why I do it. You can ask anything of me, Juliette.' He hesitated. 'If you would just do the one thing I ask of you.'

I shook my head. There was no point in going over the same argument. Nothing would induce me to leave France and her needy children, and eventually he'd have to accept this. 'You know that I want you to go home, Peter, for your safety, but you will not. So we must agree to disagree.' A specious statement, when I knew in my heart that while I continued to use him he would stay with me. My guilts were piling up – deceit, misuse, falsity of all kinds in the service of the weak and innocent.

'Now to work, Peter. Tomorrow I shall fall downstairs and sprain my ankle, and you, my assistant, will accompany me on my crutches to the Conciergerie, carrying my medical bag. The bag will be filled with items to purchase the co-operation of certain prisoners. Over a period of a few days the guards will become accustomed to your presence, and then we'll act.'

As I continued to outline the plan I could not help but notice Peter's lagging enthusiasm. However, when I asked if there was a difficulty, he denied this and begged me to continue.

I, too, had reservations. The newborn child I hoped to bring out of the prison could not be transported by the *clandestines*, whose numbers had been seriously depleted by their enemies. There was no one in their band who could take charge of such a young child, feed it and keep it quiet and hidden for the length of time it would take to reach England. I'd arranged a suitable wet nurse to take in the babe briefly, but afterwards....

As we made our preparations the following day I realized how tired I felt. The strain of past months was beginning to affect me, and I had far less energy than before I came to Paris. Of course, everyone existed under intense pressure of some kind, including those who rode the crest of the revolutionary wave, balancing precariously. For the rest of us, trying to keep our heads above water was tiring. I could see no end to this scenario, and yet I knew it all must eventually come crashing down. What occupied every mind was the question of who would survive, and what their world would be like when they washed up on it.

Peter smiled at my erratic efforts on crutches, but his face was tense as we negotiated the stairs down into the depths of the Conciergerie's hall of prisoners. He had tied back his hair and, shabby yet neat, he was the epitome of the doctor's assistant. Supposedly somewhat dull, if he were called upon to speak his accent would be attributed to his being of German descent. However, he couldn't hide his abhorrence of the fortress prison. For him, the cold grey stones clearly reflected the misery and hopelessness of countless former and present inmates. He avoided looking into faces, as if afraid of what he might see there. When I met with the women who were my co-conspirators, he stood well aside and contemplated his down-at-heel boots.

I had no time to worry about him. The soap and combs and other articles of grooming that I handed out brought smiles to the worn features of the women who cared for my prospective smuggled goods and his mother. They proudly showed me the infant limbs, unswaddled for inspection, and commented on his good sleeping habits. These last were particularly important, because he must sleep through his transportation from the prison. I could not mesmerize a child so young, and I would not attempt to administer laudanum or any other soporific.

The truly heart-wrenching part of this exercise was dealing with the mother. She lay in her cot covered with piled rags, coats, anything available, and still she shook with fever – child-birth fever, for which there was no cure.

The small cell, stuffy and dark, with the inevitable prison odour of congested humanity made worse by the woman's condition, was a sad place in which to die. At least it was cooler than the sun-baked courtyard. I wished I could have brought this woman some real comfort, but all I could offer was a future for her child.

Putting aside my sticks, I knelt beside her and felt the pulse frantically racing in her frail wrist.

'Your babe is healthy,' I assured her, bringing a smile to her cracked lips.

'*Merci, m'sieu*,' she whispered. 'When ... when will you take him?'

'In two days' time.'

'Then ... I must live for two days more, to feed him and ... to send him on to his new life.'

I could hardly bear to see the sadness in her eyes. 'Twas always a cruel thing to watch a mother's farewell to her child, with one of them about to step through death's doorway. Yet, in this case sorrow was balanced by the opportunity to cheat the State of one small victim. If I should succeed in spiriting him away into the arms of another woman who could nurture him, at least for a time, then surely a way would be found to offer him a full life.

Having done what I could to make her comfortable, I signalled to Peter to follow, and continued on my regular round of the prison. There were gaps amongst the familiar faces, more than usual. One fairy-like child was an especial favourite of mine. She insisted upon performing a dance for my enjoyment whenever I visited. Sadly, an enquiry for her brought only head-shakes. I had to bite my tongue and turn aside to control my reaction. Peter and I made a dismal couple as we left the precincts, long-faced and, in my case, awkwardly hopping between two sticks.

'That is a terrible place,' Peter said as we crossed the river and I could resume my normal pace.

'So are the streets,' I retorted. 'At least the prisoners have food and shelter while they wait.'

Peter looked shocked. 'But they're going to die!'

'So are Jaseur's playmates – those starvelings who sell themselves and eat rats.'

He was silenced, and I immediately regretted my outburst. I realized how stretched my nerves had become. The truth was that, despite my gratitude for his help, Peter's dog-like devotion was an irritant. I'd have preferred to have him stand up to me, tell me when I was overbearing or short to the point of rudeness. A good argument could clear the air.

When a memory rose of my many verbal tussles with Armand, I squashed it, ruthlessly, and invited Peter to supper.

On the third day of my supposed injury Peter carried the bag with the comfortably lined false pocket beneath. He took my sticks and waited in silent commiseration as I entered the fetid cell. There I stooped and took the infant from his mother's arms. Her grief was too great for tears. The eyes in the sunken face were like burning embers about to be extinguished. Her whispered farewell and blessing upon us both were her last words before she turned her head aside. I could do no more for her.

Fighting my emotion, I settled the sleeping babe in his strange nest and accepted a package from the women who had acted as nurses to the dying mother. It held a set of ruby buttons that would help to keep others alive. The women already wore the hopeless look of those beyond help; yet saving the child had done something for them. Perhaps it was a small spark of defiance, or simply the human need to preserve the generations to come. I inwardly saluted their courage as each touched the child in farewell then faded back into the darkness of her own cell.

Peter trembled like a *blancmanger*. He could hardly hold the bag steady, and I made him wait and take several deep breaths before stepping out into the quadrangle. I was angry with myself. I'd seen his unwillingness for this venture, although he'd denied it, and I'd been too determined to go ahead to take proper note. Now everything was jeopardized by my stupidity.

I said, 'Peter, the babe is well fed and will continue to sleep, unless handled roughly or disturbed by undue noise. You need not fear he will reveal his presence by crying.'

He swallowed and would not meet my gaze, saying, 'I'm ashamed, Juliette. You have a coward for a support, a broken reed.'

I answered him vehemently. 'No, Peter. A coward would not have continued in the face of his fear. I should have allowed for the strain of past weeks, with you living as a fugitive in a foreign land, never knowing when the moment of discovery might arrive. *Mon Dieu*, haven't my own nerves been scraped raw enough by the continual threat of denunciation for whatever reason that might occur to the rabble?' I brushed a hand over my face and forced myself to speak in a measured tone. 'I apologize for involving you in this situation, Peter, but we must go on. Your role is to act as the simple-minded bearer of my medical bag. There's no reason why you should be addressed, but if it happens I'll deal with the officials while you stand aside and look vacant.'

He straightened his shoulders and took a firmer grasp on the bag, saying grimly, 'I should be able to manage so much.'

As I'd anticipated, there was no problem with our departure – not until Peter, sweating with relief, lost his footing on the steps up to the entrance. Throwing out his arms to save himself, he let the bag go. It rose into the air, and as it sailed past I dropped my sticks and grabbed for it. By the grace of God I caught the handles and clutched it to my chest as I rolled back down to the foot of the stairs. I lay there feeling as though, for the first time in my life, I might actually swoon.

Guards came running. They picked me up and handed me my crutches. They picked up Peter and handed him the medical bag. And that miraculous baby let out not one cry. Had we killed the poor child? My wits were so addled with shock, I remembered little about our stumbling passage down the street and across the bridge. Not until we reached a hidden courtyard where we'd be unobserved did I dare to open the bag.

Two milky blue eyes looked up at me and a pair of tiny pink lips blew a bubble, followed by the most delicate of burps. I began to laugh. The babe was safe. We were safe. My laughter rose uncontrollably, and I was only brought back to my senses by Peter's shaking me. He was white-faced and a tic jumped in his cheek.

'Stop it! Stop it! Christ Almighty, Juliette! I thought we were all dead.'

'Not you, alone,' I gasped, pushing him away. 'I'm all right, Peter. You've shaken the hysterics out of me.' I tucked up the infant and partly closed the bag. 'But never again. I couldn't do that again.'

Peter just looked at me. 'I need a drink,' he said.

CHAPTER 13

IT WAS MID October, the season of sadness, with summer fading and leaves withering, and this year, with a queen about to be put to death.

Maxine was beside herself with excitement. As a foundation member of the radical female *Société des Républicaines–Révolutionnaires*, whose members had vowed to live or die in defence of the Republic, she'd recently helped move their headquarters away from the Jacobins. They had parted with acrimony, preferring the extremism and bullying tactics of the *enragés*. Maxine clearly saw herself as an agent of liberty, hunting down the nation's internal enemies. She had adopted the conspicuous uniform of red and white striped trousers with pistol or dagger tucked into the belt, plus the *bonnet rouge* formerly used only by men, and she now roamed the streets looking for trouble.

The news of the Queen's forthcoming trial was a joy to her, and she wanted me to celebrate. But I was saddened by her blood lust and, only with great difficulty, extracted myself from induction into the *Société* and the bestowal of my own pair of striped trousers. I did agree to attend a meeting as a means of satisfying Maxine that my Republican beliefs were honest. I couldn't afford her enmity. And the meeting revealed the great strength of this feminist arm of the Revolution.

The speakers made it obvious that the *Société* had joined forces with the Cordeliers to cement an advantageous working alliance, aiming towards the systematic use of terror against enemies of the Republic. By 'enemies' they meant Girondins, aristocrats, hoarders and speculators. Robespierre and the Jacobins were not mentioned, although their inimical presence was in the room.

I left shaken, unwillingly impressed, yet fearful of the strong fanatical element within the society led by women like Maxine.

Later, one afternoon, by chance I met Armand walking in the Tuileries Gardens. The sun was going down behind leafless trees and a ground mist had formed, striking chill through my clothing and leaving a moist coating on my cheeks. The bleakness of my surroundings struck me. No one now tended the flower beds or raked the gravel and gathered the fallen leaves. All was grey desolation – except in one small corner where an old man leaned over a stone pot, digging with a trowel. I paused to watch and realized that he was tending a lone rose bush. It was bare but for one last yellow bloom. A light in the wilderness, I thought, and felt my spirits lift. Nature always had her gifts, no matter how much man destroyed.

It was then I saw Armand. Although my moments for private thought, as well as beneficial exercise, were briefly snatched, I welcomed my friend with warmth. Then, to hide my too obvious delight in his company, I sought a controversial subject and hit upon the Queen's removal to the Conciergerie prior to her trial.

Armand seemed *distrait*, although he roused himself to denounce this as a political error of judgement. 'Not only a mistake,' he declared 'but needlessly cruel. The Austrian may have been stupidly greedy and ignorant of the needs of her subjects, but she's paid a heavy price with the loss of husband, family and liberty, and everything that made her royal. Do we need to take her life as well? Does it advance the Republic in any way?'

'Of course not. How you've changed, Armand. I know you approved the execution of the King.'

'That was another matter. It was necessary to remove the pivot of the monarchist support movement.' He paused. 'As you observe, I've had to revise some of my opinions. Yet, in fairness, 'tis not I who have changed, but the Revolution itself. It's been taken over by ruthless men insane with power, and I fear all may be brought to ruin.'

Deep sadness underlay his dismay. I'd come to recognize the genuine patriotism behind his apparent enthusiasm for a blood-thirsty regime. He'd had such high hopes for the betterment of society, and truly believed in the need to tear down the social structure in order to replace it with something better. However, along with many others, he'd been deceived. The ruthless sector, headed by Robespierre and the Jacobins, had ambushed the more moderate element and taken over and distorted the push for freedom. The great Revolution had descended into nothing more than a tool for the spreading of terror.

We'd been pacing the gravelled walks for several minutes before Armand stopped and turned to me with a look of such gravity that I knew this was no chance meeting.

'What is it, Armand?' I'd used his baptismal name for the first time!

'I need your help, Juliette. I pray that you can help me—' He trailed off, as if uncertain how to continue.

Anything, I thought, but said, 'Tell me.'

'I have a niece, a beloved child of my sister, Victorine.'

He was sweating, despite the evening chill. He removed his hat briefly to wipe his forehead, then continued, 'She married into the aristocracy, a family of note in the south, and was blessed with this little daughter. I love the child, and she's the darling of my sister's heart.'

My own heart contracted as if a cold hand had cupped and squeezed it. I knew what was coming.

He kept his tone deliberate and even. 'There was a peasant uprising in their province and the family was taken and imprisoned. My brother-in-law has already been executed, and Victorine and little Clara are now lodged in the Carmes prison in terrible conditions.' Suddenly his voice broke. 'Before God, I've done everything possible to secure their release, but I've failed. Now I turn to you, Juliette, as my last hope. Will you … can you help me?'

When I recall those moments, the conflicting emotions that swept through me like a cyclonic wind, I wonder how I ever stayed on my feet. The pity I felt for Armand, tortured by his powerlessness; my despair over my lack of contact with the Carmes; my delight in his need for my help – even disappointment that he'd never shared with me any information about his family – all overwhelmed me.

For once, with a huge effort, I succeeded in hiding my thoughts. Armand's gaze hadn't wavered as he waited for me to respond, to say that I would help. And I could not.

'Armand, you know I'd do anything in my power—'

'Don't … I beg you; don't say you cannot do anything. You've done it for others.' He grasped my shoulders, squeezing painfully in his anxiety.

If I could only have promised to save his sister and her beloved child.

He saw the answer in my face, only inches from his own. 'Juliette!'

'Oh, Armand, I'm sorry. 'Tis impossible. I'm not allowed into the Carmes, or any prison other than the Conciergerie.'

'If I could arrange entry for you, could you practice your

magic there? I've never asked you how you spirited those children away, but now I must know. You have to tell me if there's a way.'

His eyes held me with the force of magnets, willing me, demanding, pleading.

Could it be done? If I could gain admission, and permission to treat patients, would there be the opportunity to practice my mesmerism on the two? But two, and one of them an adult!

I gently released myself from his hold and stepped back. 'I don't know,' I said, at last. 'Have you seen your sister?'

'Yes. I'm permitted to attend those in need of surgery, and I can usually spend a few minutes with her. May I tell her there is hope?'

I'd have given years of my life to relieve the strain that wrenched his nerves and had aged him immeasurably, but I could not give false hope. 'It depends upon so many things. I can demonstrate to you the method whereby we trick the authorities into thinking a person is dead, but I've never taken out a living adult. Is your sister a big woman?'

He nodded. 'Since her fall from a horse she's been unable to walk far and has gained weight. She's very heavy.' He hesitated. 'She suffers from the dropsy and her heart is unreliable.'

My spirits sank even lower. 'Well, little Clara. How old is she?'

His smile was a pale replica of itself. At least it was a smile in a face grown so dear to me. 'She's a diminutive six-year-old, as bright as a gold louis and mischievous as a monkey.'

'She sounds delightful. An intelligent child can be more easily persuaded to succumb to mesmerism.'

'Aah! So that's your method.' The curiosity of a professional peeped through for a moment, then faded as he registered my meaning. 'Are you saying that Victorine presents a difficulty?'

'Well, yes. Still, I may think of a way around it. Armand, the first of our many difficulties will be gaining permission for me to enter the Carmes, not just once, but several times. Can you do it?'

Again his hat came off, this time to allow him to run a hand through his hair, as if this would somehow clear his thinking. He said, 'I can but try. No, I will do it! Once they are free I can smuggle them out of Paris and to the coast. There are plenty of sea captains taking money to transport refugees.'

We talked a little longer, both of us striving to appear confident, assuring each other that we could devise an infallible escape plan for his sister and niece. Yet, even with access to the Carmes prison, the onus would still be upon me. It was a heavy burden.

When Peter called in the evening and found me brooding over Mère Poisson's kitchen hearth, he instantly perceived my mood.

'What ails you, my dear Juliette? Is there something I can do for you?'

I'd already determined never again to ask for Peter's help with an escape plot. His nerves simply would not stand another such episode as the last. He had, however, proved invaluable in the matter of transporting the newborn babe to safety. An acquaintance from the days of the *salon* had emerged from hiding, along with his family, and with passports to leave Paris and travel to Spain. For a sum, and in recognition of the infant's noble name, they'd agreed to take him along with their own child's wet-nurse, and to raise him as their own. It was a happy ending to a sad situation.

Gently brushing aside Peter's concern, I was about to suggest a visit to the local wineshop when Armand arrived, and Jaseur led him straight in. Not noticing Peter sitting in the shadows, Armand plunged into excited speech.

'I've managed to secure a pass for you to the Carmes prison.

You will be able to meet with Victorine and discuss a possible means of escape for her—' He broke off, flicking a wary glance at Peter as he rose and came into the light.

I said, 'It's all right. Peter has already helped in several escapes. He'll not betray us.' All the same, I pushed back my chair and placed myself between them. There was hostility in the air.

Armand did not look convinced. However, he merely nodded stiffly. But Peter's whole stance was that of a hackled terrier whose bone was in jeopardy.

I stifled a smile and turned back to Armand. ''Tis good news indeed.'

'No!' Peter burst out. 'The time has come for you to abandon such risks. There's no guarantee there will be no mishap, such as occurred recently. I can think of several possibilities—'

'Peter, stop it. I appreciate your concern, but I'm the one best placed to arrange these things.'

'Why should it be you, always you, who assumes this burden?' He glared at Armand. 'This is *your* affair. You deal with it.'

Armand's frown darkened. 'If I could do so, I would. I have no desire to drag Juliette into danger. Nothing is decided, as yet. And she will not be unsupported. Naturally, I shall be a part of whatever scheme is devised.'

Peter fulminated. I was reminded of a bubbling kettle about to blow its lid. 'Did she tell you about the last time?' he asked. 'Did she tell you how we both came within a knife blade of discovery?' His fair skin had flushed and his clenched fists shook with the desire to release some of his tension, most probably on Armand's chin.

Armand simply registered impatience. He was about to speak when I interrupted.

'Both of you listen to me,' I said. 'The decision is mine. I shall assess the situation and do nothing until I can be reasonably assured of success. Peter, if you can't stay calm, I must ask you to leave. In fact, 'twould be best if you both were to leave now and give me time to consider the situation.'

They didn't like that. No doubt Peter resented his inability to sway my determination, but his naturally pliable disposition left him open to pressure from a stronger will. His jealousy also placed him at a disadvantage. Armand was a different case. I could see the repressed anger and need for action in every line of his face. He wanted to be in control. The masculine desire to head the charge was strong in him. However, I knew he'd not risk an argument in front of Peter, one in which he could find himself worsted. He would bide his time and return later.

As the third party in this uncomfortable meeting, I just wanted to be left alone to think. My love for Armand didn't blind me to his overpowering nature, or the fact that his emotional involvement could be dangerous; while Peter in his present state was simply a nuisance.

The two men finally accepted their dismissal with reasonable grace and, relieved, I sat down to supper with Jaseur. It had occurred to me that Armand's jubilation was premature. A pass for me to enter the Carmes was one thing; jurisdiction over the prisoners, and the right to sign out a corpse was another. I needed to investigate the situation thoroughly before I could even begin to make a plan.

CHAPTER 14

I'D NOT EASILY forget my first day in Paris, with my introduction to the mob's excesses. The walls of the former Carmelite convent now known as Les Carmes were still stained with blood from the September Massacres. Not surprisingly, Jaseur refused to go anywhere near the place.

It wasn't the most feared of the revolutionary gaols, such as La Force in the Marais district, or the dreaded Temple, but conditions were very much worse than in the Conciergerie. I was shocked to find as many as eighteen women packed into a cell, creating the perfect breeding ground for gaol fever. There were also many more representatives of the lower classes, from seamstresses to prostitutes to peasant wives trapped in the city. I couldn't imagine why they would be accused of sedition. Most were simply frightened and bewildered victims of the State juggernaut.

Upon my request for the *ci-devant* Vicomtesse Victorine de Montferrier, I was directed to a corner in the courtyard where I found a sick woman struggling to hold on to life. Wheezing and dropsical, she sat like an overstuffed sack, her face raised to the pale autumn sun as if desperate to absorb what energy was available. With her brittle, greying hair and her features distorted in the folds of flesh, she might have been in her fiftieth year, rather than her thirtieth. Yet she addressed me in a voice of such beauty that at first I didn't realize it was she who spoke.

'M'sieu le Docteur, how kind of you to call. *Hélas*, I fear there is little you can do for me. But pray be seated.' It was the voice of a dove, of small bells, of – I almost thought – an angel. Which was absurd. I'd absolutely no knowledge of angelic tones, and this was one highly visible human being. Nevertheless, I was enchanted. I took my seat beside her, looking into eyes deeply embedded, yet vital, reflecting a strong and serene inner spirit, despite every breath being a strain, despite her desperate situation.

She clasped fat little hands in her lap and said, 'So, you are the one.'

'The one?' My puzzlement was tinged with momentary anxiety. Had Armand given away my secret to his sister? I still had the greatest fear of being revealed, accidentally or otherwise, and having my usefulness destroyed. There were people dependent upon me, with nowhere else to turn for trained medical help, for a handful of sous to keep the roof overhead, to feed a starving child. The sisters did what they could, and there were a few benefactors who donated time and expertise. However, 'few' was the operative word in a city on the brink of anarchy. So I looked to the sick woman for an explanation.

'My brother speaks of you, often.' She took a gasping breath.

'Speaks of me?' I echoed. I probably looked as vacant as a cow chewing cud.

She laughed, and three chins wobbled as her little eyes disappeared from sight. 'How discourteous of me. I beg your forgiveness.' She paused between each few words to regain her breath, but nothing could destroy the flow of that mellifluous voice. It warmed me, drawing me in, making me a welcome confidante.

'Your brother is my friend,' I said, still cautious.

'Of course. He told me to expect you. He said you would bring some kind of news for me ... Juliette.'

I glanced around to be sure we were not overheard. 'Comtesse—'

'Victorine, please, as a friend.'

We might well have become friends, in time, had there been time. But I'd seen at once that she could never sustain any sort of excitement or strain. Death already had his mark upon her. Surely Armand knew. Or did he refuse to recognize something he found unbearable?

In that moment I forgave him for revealing my secret to his sister. 'Yes, I'm Juliette Roussel.'

'And a doctor. How wonderful to possess the skill to help many people.' She smiled with a look of such hope.

Knowing that the only way I could help her would be to save her child, I gathered my thoughts and explained my smuggling system and its successful outcome, so far.

She was delighted. 'Armand said you were clever, as well as beautiful and intelligent. I cannot express my depth of gratitude for your help.'

He thought me beautiful and intelligent! He'd talked about me! I hugged the thought close, before putting it aside for later consideration. This was the time to face Victorine with honesty.

'There are difficulties. For the present, there's little I can do beyond testing young Clara for her susceptibility to mesmerism. I've no authority within this prison. Still, I will do all in my power to obtain it.'

This was clearly a devastating blow and Victorine's breathing worsened as she struggled not to collapse. I gave her an infusion of digitalis and hellebore and supported her into a half-lying position, waiting until she'd recovered. When several of the women nearby rushed to help, I assured them that the

Comtesse needed only air and rest. They drifted away, but not far. She was their friend and I was an unknown quantity.

Eventually she sat up, her expression strained, although she spoke kindly. 'I pray you, do not be distressed. 'Twas not your fault that my stupid heart reacted badly. I know you will use your best endeavours for us.'

'You have my promise.' I wanted to be more reassuring, but couldn't bring myself to give false hope. Armand had already done so, and I would not add to it. Poor Armand. Clearly he needed to sustain a strong, loving link between his sister and himself, even at the expense of reality.

When I asked to meet Clara, she was brought to me by one of the watching women. They were happy to serve Victorine's disability, most likely because her nature didn't demand service.

Her little daughter was sweet and biddable, and appeared eminently suitable as a subject. However, once that had been decided I knew I must speak of Victorine herself. As I searched for the right words she forestalled me, in the forthright, yet gentle manner that I was beginning to recognize.

'You need not concern yourself with me, Juliette. There Armand is asking for the impossible. *Regardez moi!*' She spread her hands ruefully.

The poor woman's upper body bulged so that her arms couldn't even fall straight by her sides, and the swelling of her ankles gave her the 'elephant legs' characteristic of her illness. Her weight would cause huge difficulty in the way of transport.

'Your brother would never forgive me—' I began.

'Tsk. Armand is a dreamer, when these times call for a realist. He's also very stubborn.' She sighed. 'First, we must see Clara safe.'

Armand a dreamer? Clearly there were many more layers to his personality than I'd seen or guessed at. Or was this the fond, but erroneous thinking of a loving sister?

Once again those sparkling eyes disappeared in crinkles of amusement.

'You do not believe me? I assure you, 'twas ever so, from childhood until he found the world was no place for dreamers to expose themselves. He was eventually forced to don a disguise, a protective shield that circumstances have hardened into an iron cast.'

I longed to ask 'what circumstances?' and I suppose my wretchedly revealing face asked for me.

Victorine shook her greying head. ''Tis not for me to tell you what he has not. One woman betrayed him, and I will never do it. I will tell you that he has never spoken of anyone in such glowing terms as he uses to describe his "Little Docteur Juliette".'

'I'm five feet and five inches tall,' I blurted, with a feeling of mingled pleasure and annoyance. After all, Armand topped me by no more than four or five inches. However, the pleasure was uppermost. Such a crumb of comfort, to have one's height commented upon! Was I so desperate for his notice? And had I not already decided after a whole sleepless night not to allow myself to love in a romantic, passionate way? Yet I had to ask one vital question.

'I'd never want you to violate your brother's confidence, but could you just tell me whether this "one woman" who betrayed him is his wife?'

She hesitated. 'Once she was. Now she is dead.'

'Thank you for telling me.' I felt numb. He had loved another woman with such intensity that her betrayal had altered his whole nature. And the numbness gave way to a surge of rage. I knew I could have struck that woman, had she stood before me. I suppose Victorine saw it all. There was no point in my trying to hide what must be obvious to her.

She took my hand, and her lovely voice was gentle as she

said, 'He is a good man and worthy of your affection, my dear. I pray you, do not hurt him.'

'No. There is no possibility … he does not feel … we are good friends and colleagues—'

She merely smiled. 'Let me tell you some things about Armand. We are close in age and shared many experiences in our youth.'

I knew it was a mistake, knew that I was inviting future pain and sorrow, yet I could not resist. I might never have another opportunity to learn about the boy within the grown man, the dreamer who had donned armour against the world and could not now remove it.

I stayed as long as the guards would permit, then left reluctantly, with a feeling that time was running out. All the way home I pondered the difficulty of facing Armand with no real answers. Any attempt at escape from the Carmes was out of the question. I'd been told from the moment when I applied for my position that the Conciergerie was the only prison where I could work. Unless Armand had enormous influence, that would not change.

Then there was the absolute impossibility of saving Victorine. How did I say: 'Your sister is too sick and too heavy to move?' Or worse: 'Your sister cannot live beyond another year.'

I hated the thought of failing them. Victorine was the first person of rank whom I'd liked upon sight. That is, apart from Camille, my friend from childhood. No doubt Victorine's bourgeois upbringing had helped to form a naturally sweet nature. She was an admirable woman with the courage to face reality and place her hopes upon the survival of her child. For the sake of all three, there had to be a way of bringing little Clara to safety.

Although dreading my meeting with Armand that night, I found that I'd underestimated him. He'd gone to Danton for help, and his friend had not failed him.

'George has arranged for my sister's transfer to the Conciergerie,' Armand said, steering me into Mère Poisson's kitchen, where he seemed to be perfectly at home.

It was the cosiest place in the house, possibly in the neighbourhood. For here my kind landlady had gathered her last remaining treasured possessions, those not yet disposed of for basic necessities. She might have come down in the world, but in this one room she had managed to maintain a level of comfort more often found in a long-established farmhouse than in the slums of Saint-Antoine. There might be cracked window panes and crazy, tilted floorboards, but there were also the dresser with its plate rack, now empty, the table scrubbed white with use, the two sturdy chairs, each with a hand-worked cushion, and the clock on the mantel over the fireplace, its painted china face and pointed iron hands dust free and shining. All were proud mementos of better days.

As a frequent visitor to the section's poor, Armand basked in Mère Poisson's approval, and there certainly could be no safer place than this for plotting. This we did, while Jaseur guarded the door against any accidental callers.

We drew our chairs comfortably before the fire, but Armand still looked worried.

'What is it?' I asked. 'Are you not pleased to have Danton's help?'

The firelight flickered, sending shadows dancing across his face, altering his expression from moment to moment. Had I imagined his look of strain?

'Of course I'm pleased, and grateful to George. Yet I fear for him. He is ill, Juliette, with a terrible weariness. 'Tis as though he can no longer bear the load he carries.'

'I don't understand. He is a great bull of a man, with enormous vitality.'

Armand shook his head. 'He has suffered many disappointments. I think, too, this business of the Queen's indictment is a blow to his prestige. George had hoped to use her to bargain with foreign powers, you know. And he pities her. He speaks of her as "that poor woman" in the same way as he grieves for "our poor country". He has changed, immeasurably.'

My sympathy was limited, and I mentally shrugged. Danton was not my concern. I had not liked him or the things he stood for, although I could pity him, even while turning to the more important work in hand – the rescue of those he'd helped to put in jeopardy.

Armand said more cheerfully, 'Thanks to him, at least, our main difficulty has been overcome.'

''Tis early for rejoicing. There are several more challenges before us. Firstly, the transfer of the Queen to the Conciergerie has meant extra security measures have been put in place. The prison is locked tight before dusk, with no one permitted entry or exit. Clara's rescue will be carried out in full daylight while the guards are alert.'

'But the child will sleep?'

'Of course. However, it means I cannot draw attention by accompanying her to the burial pit. Nor can I find bearers whom I can trust, even if well bribed. My story of grave robbing wears thin, and they think it too perilous.' I paused, thinking ahead. 'You know that I no longer have the support of the *clandestines*? Those not already caught and executed have left the country.'

He would not be discouraged. 'There will be ways around these difficulties. I'll give my mind to them.' He rose from the fireside and began to walk the floor, stopping when he reached me. 'Juliette … about Victorine.'

I looked up at him and was caught in his gaze. All at once I recalled Victorine's comments, and felt myself blushing. I turned my face to the fire and watched the incandescent coals shift and flare, knowing that the heat I felt came from within me.

'Juliette, what did she say?'

Say? I thought. She said so much. Yet I knew what he asked. The moment I'd dreaded had arrived and I had no alternative but to give him the truth.

'Armand, I cannot help Victorine. Knowing how much she means to you—' I faltered, made myself look up, steeling myself against his disappointment in me. 'If I could find a way ... she knows 'tis not possible. She said as much.'

He flung up a hand. 'Pray say no more.' His face was so drawn.

I'd seldom felt as desolate as I did at that moment.

Then I felt a hand on my shoulder, the pressure warm and comforting.

'You should not blame yourself, Juliette. I know my sister, and can guess at her decision.' I heard a faint sigh. 'She is as stubborn as a balky mule and, once decided upon a course, will not be shifted at the point of a pike.'

'She said the same of you.' A huge weight lifted off my heart. I should have credited him with more understanding.

'No doubt. There have been some rare disagreements between us.' His brief smile faded. 'Juliette, what think you of her health?'

I avoided his eyes. 'She is a very sick woman, Armand. You must know.'

'Yes, I know it.' He removed his hand and began pacing again.

I felt bereft, as if some warm part of myself had gone cold. So much for my plan to starve my love until it had shrunk to an apple pip. It fed on every glance, on every word he spoke. I could not banish it even when dealing with matters of life and death.

Still, I fought to suppress all thought of myself, and together we plotted well into the night by fire and candle. And when the first light through the window paled these into insignificance we had our plan.

CHAPTER 15

IT HAD BEEN agreed that Jaseur's little handcart would form the bier for Clara, as he would be quite strong enough to push it. This did away with the need for bearers, and allowed Armand to wait for us in his carriage one street away from the guard's eyes, ready to scoop up the child and disappear.

Armand was not happy with his role. He'd have preferred to take the more dangerous part, but he knew it was impossible. I alone could send Clara into a sleeping trance and formally declare her dead. Possibly Peter's jibe, that Armand was prepared to allow a woman to do his dangerous work, had left its mark. Still, I respected his willingness to stand aside and allow me to carry on without any further objection. It meant that he saw me as an equal.

Jaseur was thrilled to be included in the enterprise and had to be restrained from practising his role in the street with one of his friends playing the corpse. However, time was short. With the Queen's trial about to commence, who knew what unexpected changes might soon be made in the prison routine? Two days after our plotting was finalized, we acted.

With everyone else dismissed from the cell, I set myself to induce Clara's 'sleep'. My heart bled for Victorine as she 'laid out' her small daughter in the handcart, which Jaseur had thoughtfully lined with a ragged coverlet.

'We will take the greatest care of her,' I murmured.

Victorine wiped her wet cheeks. 'I know it. *Hélas*! Words are not enough. My gratitude goes beyond them. You will honour me by accepting this small gift in my memory.' She placed in my hand an exquisite miniature painted on ivory and mounted with diamonds. It portrayed a younger, smiling Victorine and her baby daughter, their cheeks pressed together, their curls mingling. It was a portrayal of love.

I felt tears springing. 'I shall see you again, to tell you how Clara fares.'

She regarded me steadily. 'God willing. But my final days are even now being noted by the recording angel. You know this, dear Juliette. And I am content. Clara will live and … and I pray that she will remember me.'

'Armand will keep your memory forever fresh in her mind, while I shall treasure your gift until Clara is grown, and then pass it into her keeping.'

Victorine stooped her ungainly body to clasp the sleeping child for the last time. I turned away, unable to watch. When a kiss descended on my cheek, I started.

'That was for Armand. You will convey it to him when you hand him this letter?' The dark eyes, buried in the creases of her swollen face, sparkled momentarily with mischief, before grief clouded them once more.

I could only nod. Placing the letter in my cuff, along with the precious miniature, I grasped both her hands briefly, then motioned to Jaseur to proceed. The three of us walked the length of the courtyard, slowly, in deference to Victorine's laboured breathing. I wondered how many more times I'd cross these flagstones with the body of a sleeping child, accompanied by a heart-broken mother. It grew no easier with each one. Time after time I felt a part of me wrenched away. So much sorrow, so much pain. The tearing asunder of families was one of the worst

FRANCES BURKE

aspects of the Revolution. To many, a swift and sudden death would have been preferable.

Finally we reached the gates into the prisoners' hall. The guard undid the lock, motioning Victorine back, and Jaseur and me through. I looked down and saw Clara twitch.

Victorine grasped my arm. 'Mon Dieu! I had hoped this would not happen.' Her anguished voice was just a whisper.

Horrified, I whispered back, 'What is it?' We'd gone too far to stop. Already the guard was looking in our direction, prepared to escort us to the recording clerk's table.

Victorine's voice shook so badly, I could scarcely make out her words. 'As a babe she was subject to an intermittent palsy, but I believed she had grown beyond it. No doubt the excitement of a supposed visit to her uncle has brought it on again.'

'You did not think to warn me? Oh, Victorine.' More likely Clara had sensed her mother's tension and grief at their parting. Children are highly attuned to such things. But if I'd known about the palsy I could have induced Clara to control the tremors, such is the power of the hypnotic trance. Now it was too late.

Clara twitched again, and I saw the dawning fear in Jaseur's face.

Victorine's expression had hardened into determination. She gave Jaseur a push and said, 'Go! Now!'

He stumbled forward with the cart and the gates closed behind us. I looked back to see the massive figure of Victorine lumbering back towards the cells at an impossible pace. She would kill herself, I thought, even as I hurried after Jaseur.

The clerk's table loomed. The guards stepped forward. Time slowed until I felt I waded through a sea of molasses, with my boots needing to be unglued before each step. We reached the desk, the clerk opened his ledger. I gave the name. Clara twitched.

Jaseur dropped the handles of the cart, snatched up the clerk's silver inkwell, and took to his heels. Through the hall, out the door and down the steps he sped, leaving the guards momentarily stunned. As they awoke and set off in full cry of 'Stop, thief!' a terrific row erupted from the women's courtyard. I heard a voice screaming: 'The Queen! The Queen escapes. *À moi! À moi!*'

The clerk leaped up, overturning the table, and the remaining guards joined him in the rush to the gates. A bell began to toll. Other voices took up the cry: 'Guards! Help! To arms. The Queen escapes.'

I picked up the cart handles and hurried out the door. Turning sharply to the left, I flew over those cobbles as if with winged feet, and around the corner to where Armand's carriage waited.

He sprang to meet me, his face urgent with worry. The bells and shouting were a clear warning to be gone.

'What's happened? Are you pursued?' He scooped up Clara as he spoke and placed her within the carriage. I scrambled in after her crying, 'Go, for the love of God!' He slammed the door and climbed to the driver's seat. The horses, made restive by the noise, leaped forward, and we were away.

I hung from the window and shouted, 'Look out for Jaseur. He headed for the bridge with the guards chasing him.'

It was then I heard the shots.

No! They couldn't shoot a child. However, they would a thief. I leaned further from the window in an effort to see ahead. It was still daylight, but the carriage bounced, causing me to bang my head on the roof until I had to withdraw. I sat back clutching Clara to keep her from slipping to the floor.

We reached the bridge and I felt my heart contract at the sight of two guards leaning over the parapet scanning the turgid waters below. One pointed and laughed, and they turned away to walk back in the direction of the Conciergerie.

Jaseur had gone into the river. Had he been shot? Could he survive the current and the dangerous flotsam of the waterway? Or would his body be washed up on some muddy bank miles beyond the city? I sank back on the carriage seat with Clara clasped tightly to me, and wept.

The following day was one of the most miserable I've ever known.

With Clara tucked into Mère Poisson's bed, still in her trance-like sleep, I returned to the Conciergerie. I was torn, longing to join the search for Jaseur, yet needing to know what had happened back in the prison and to reassure Victorine. Clara was a good subject for deep and prolonged trance. I hadn't wakened her for the simple reason that she would find herself among strangers and be frightened. Armand had joined in the search for Jaseur and might not return before nightfall, while Mère Poisson, whose reproachful gaze made me writhe, had agreed to care for the child.

So, with reluctant steps, I went back to the prison that morning. Surprisingly, calm prevailed. The guard had not been increased. I'd expected to find all sorts of restrictions in place. The clerk, a bilious-looking man with an equally sour manner was reinstated at his table. I noted the new inkwell of plain horn before him. He looked up at me as I passed and said, 'Citoyen Docteur, it seems you were unfortunate in your choice of assistant. You should take more care not to bring a thief into these precincts.'

I put on a shamefaced air. 'You are right, citoyen. I've since found that he stole from me, as well. However, he has paid with his life, or so I hear.'

He nodded and turned back to his ledger. It seemed clear that Clara's name had been marked off and there was no problem there. Just as Jaseur had been dismissed as another worthless body, a nameless thief gone to the bottom of the Seine.

As I waited for the guard to unlock the gate to the women's yard, my reluctance to enter came close to paralysis. Victorine would have suffered a thousand times over during the night. I could reassure her as to her child's safety, although how Armand would get her to England and to her *émigré* relatives I could not imagine. I'd trodden this path so often. Once again I must face a bereft mother, this time a woman I cared about, whose grieving touched me deeply. Despite our brief acquaintance we had both immediately recognized our emotional kinship. I did not want to face Victorine and see the ravage to her soul.

I did not have to. Candles had been lit in the dark cell and women knelt in prayer at each end of Victorine's bed – her bier. In death the swollen skin of her face had melted back to display a finely sculpted nose, a smooth brow and lips seeming to smile in contentment. The sweep of lashes, long hidden, graced a skin as fine as vellum. Victorine had been a beautiful woman, and was beautiful once again.

I said to one of the watchers, 'When did she die, and of what cause?'

The woman rose and led me outside. In the yard she turned sunken eyes on me and said, 'She died to save her daughter. I was at the gate when you took the child through. I saw what was about to happen. The Comtesse did the only thing she could to draw attention away from you. She ran through the court screaming that the Queen was escaping, that there was a great plot to break into the prison and release her.'

I nodded slowly. 'Of course. The authorities could never afford such an escape. They would be galvanized by the mere thought.'

'The guards descended upon us like an avenging horde of Mongols. But by the time it had been proved a false alarm, you had escaped and—' She halted.

I finished for her. 'And Victorine, Vicomtesse de Montferrier, mother of Clara, had died. Her heart could never have sustained such an effort, running like that, screaming, doing everything she could to draw attention.'

'She lived but a few moments from the time she collapsed. I heard her whisper that now Clara would live.' The woman's eyes held mine. 'No one else heard her. Your secret is safe.'

I nodded my thanks. There was nothing more to be said.

I continued to carry out my duties. There were still the sick and the needy who called upon me, as well as the arrangements for disposal of Victorine's body. I accompanied her all the way to the grave pit, and was forced to watch as she was tipped into the charnel pile and covered in lime. I said a brief, silent prayer for this courageous woman, then set off for home with lagging steps.

We'd been so fortunate in one way, and sustained such loss in another: Victorine dead, most probably adjudged insane by the keepers of the records; Clara lying in limbo, her future uncertain; Jaseur missing, most likely drowned. And tonight I must face Armand with news of his loss, not unexpected, but too soon.

He returned after dark. I looked up from stirring the soup pot over the fire to see him enter and throw himself down wearily at the table. His sombre expression told his tale. Jaseur had not been found.

Mère Poisson flung her apron over her face and began to rock on her stool, while I stood helplessly wondering what I could possibly say. The room was silent save for the crackle of the fire. I searched for the right words. There were none. A boy had died that a girl might live, and I had yet to tell the man I loved with every breath of my being that his beloved sister, too, was gone.

We might have sat there for an age had not the door flown back with a crash, shaking the pepper pot from the shelf and bringing us to our feet. Peter stood there, triumphant, his arm supporting the most bedraggled imp imaginable.

'Jaseur!' We flew to him, the three of us all but knocking him down.

'What happened to you?'

'Where was he?'

'How did you find him?'

'What did you do with the inkwell, you young rascal?'

That last question stood out. We stopped babbling and looked at Armand in amazement.

Jaseur let out a hoot of laughter. 'I lost it in the river. Isn't it the stupidest thing?'

Armand gave him a mock cuff over the ear and pushed him into the more solid of the two chairs by the hearth. 'Let me look at you. You smell like a water rat, but you appear to be whole.'

Jaseur grinned wearily, apparently enjoying this treatment. And while his mother hovered, anxious, yet respectful of a doctor's priority, I turned to Peter.

Impulsively, I held out my hands to him. 'How can I thank you, my friend? I could not have borne to lose the lad.'

Peter's grasp was too intense, and I could see from his expression that only the presence of the others restrained him.

'I would do anything for you,' he said in a low voice and, as I withdrew my hands, added, 'Jaseur is important to us all. He's a rascal, but with the kind of courage and ingenuity needed to make a good man.'

'I agree, if only he is given the opportunity.' And what hope was there of that, I thought, with our world in its current uproar?

Having finished his examination, Armand pronounced his patient to be ready for washing, food and bed. Leaving him to his mother's ministrations, he said to Peter. 'Englishman, I salute you. You have saved the day.'

Peter flushed bright red and raised a deprecating hand. 'No such thing. I merely came across the lad trudging home along the river-bank. He had the sense to hold on to a barrel stave and let the current take him, then fished himself out of an eddy a few miles downstream. As you see, he is very tired and very dirty, and entirely whole.'

If my smile had been any wider it would have split my face in two. 'Then the guards missed him!'

'Not a hole in him,' Armand agreed. 'This calls for wine.' He headed for the door, his former weariness slipping from him like an untied cloak.

Although it went against every feeling, I prepared to thrust another burden upon him. 'Armand,' I called. 'I'll come with you. I have something of a private nature to say to you.'

As he opened the door for me I was aware of Peter's gaze following us. Mère Poisson was far too occupied to notice.

Out in the cold street Armand was barely discernible in the faint moonlight, but I heard the concern in his voice.

'What is it, Juliette? Is Clara ill?'

'No. She sleeps, and I will wake her when you are ready.' I paused. ''Tis too soon for her to learn what happened. However, you must know the truth. Armand, I'm bitterly sorry to tell you that Victorine is dead.' I wanted to weep for him. I wanted to take his head down on to my shoulder and comfort him. I had not the right.

He stood rock still. For two or three long minutes we stood there with the wind blowing the street dirt around our ankles and finding its way inside our coats with icy fingers that presaged the first snow. Eventually he said, 'Tell me.'

And I did, exactly as it all happened. When I had finished, he took my cold hands in his and brought them to his equally chilled lips. They seared me like ice from the depths of a frozen lake, and I snatched them away.

'Don't,' I said. 'I still feel that I failed. In time I would surely have found a way to save her ... somehow.'

'My dear, we had agreed, there was no way. 'Twas Victorine's choice to make the sacrifice. She had the right. I did but try to thank you without words. There *are* no words. You are a heroine.'

Now my whole face burned, and I was thankful for the darkness to hide it. He was too gracious. He had called me 'dear'. I'd rather he'd berated me. I needed to push him from me, from my thoughts, my longings. This love that I must destroy was a killing pain, and I did not know how much longer I could bear it.

Dimly, I heard him say something about the wine, and we set off together into the night. Yet I felt more alone than I'd ever been.

CHAPTER 16

I SOON HAD no time to worry about myself. By the following morning I had two very sick people in my care. Jaseur had swallowed water from a river that was little more than a sewer and had developed a raging fever. At the same time, his mother collapsed from the strain of worry over her boy.

Moving Jaseur out of the kitchen nook into his mother's room left no space for Clara, who awoke to find herself in a strange household, with only her Uncle Armand to greet her. Her immediate request to be returned to her mother was something I could hardly face. I did the best I could, cuddling and caressing and explaining about the angels wanting *maman* to be with them, but I eventually had to leave her crying in Armand's arms and return to my several problems.

My most serious concern was for Jaseur, whose malnourished little body struggled with the inward fire threatening to consume him. He needed constant care, and I was grateful for Peter's assistance. He watched over the boy when I took my rest, and willingly turned himself into a cook/housekeeper in a role reversal that I'd normally have found amusing.

This also gave me time to make intermittent calls behind Mère Poisson's modestly curtained bedside to treat her. However, my spirits sank when I looked at her grey face and listened to her rasping breath. Her condition was grave, and although I believed she'd eventually rise from her bed, she would not regain her full health. The draught through the ill-fitting window and beneath a door that had never hung straight did not help either invalid. I kept them both bundled up and a fire going in the room, despite the huge cost, and raided my medical supplies as if there were no tomorrow.

Armand also coped with a heavy load. He stayed as long as he could with Clara, poor, bewildered infant, but at times was forced to leave her in the care of his landlady's daughter. The young woman was, happily, both clean and fond of children. Less fortunate was her devotion to her mother's lodger. This created some awkwardness. His anecdotes concerning his efforts to placate Suzette whilst avoiding an embarrassing scuffle whenever they met did amuse me, as they were meant to do; and his brief visits to Jaseur usually left the boy chuckling.

Mère Poisson soon returned to her kitchen fireside, simply as observer and commentator on Peter's cooking capabilities. Much as she wanted to help nurse her boy, it was impossible, given her weakened condition.

Armand also volunteered to explain my absence from my job at the Conciergerie and take care of any urgent needs there. I was glad enough to be absent on the day of the Queen's execution.

Matters continued in this way for more than ten days while I fought for Jaseur's life and won. It was a near thing, and there was little enough left of him by the time he could sit up and be cheeky once more.

His first thought was for the fate of his little cart, which I had to admit had been lost.

'Some rotten thief took it!' he exclaimed, thin fingers plucking agitatedly at his coverlet.

'We'll get you another one,' I said, wanting to calm him.

'I think not.' Armand spoke from behind, startling me.

I turned swiftly. 'You're back early today. Is something amiss?' I searched his dear face for any sign of debility. Jaseur's fever was of the contagious kind. Many in the medical profession mocked the notion, but I believed that there was a whole class of ills capable of passing from one person to another in a continuous chain until, for some unknown reason, a link snapped and the disease died off.

Jaseur's voice took on an invalid whine. 'Why can't I have a new cart? I could build one myself from old bits and pieces – a bigger and better one.'

Armand smiled. 'I believe you could, Jaseur, yet 'twould be unwise to exert yourself just yet. Juliette, is Mère Poisson well enough for us to hold a conference? There is a serious matter to discuss. I want Peter there, also.'

'I will look to her now, although I do believe she grows a little stronger every day. And no, Jaseur, you may not join us. If you try to stand you will fall over.' I handed him the reader that I'd purchased for him and had used to increase his word skills. 'If you can read to me one whole page when I return, you shall have an egg for supper.'

I accompanied Armand downstairs, worrying over the 'serious matter'. What more was about to befall us?

Peter left the inevitable savoury pot he was stirring, and when Mère Poisson joined us at the table with a glass of wine to support her, Armand gave us his news.

'It seems the word is out for the capture of Jaseur. The liberation of the silver inkwell was only the latest in a series of escapades, of thefts and pranks aimed at the local National Guard. He has earned a reputation, and I fear that, if recognized, he'll be captured and dealt with severely.'

I felt my face blanch. I knew what that meant in a society now crying 'treason' for any sort of crime, even juvenile theft.

Mère Poisson moaned and dropped her wineglass. I laid a

comforting hand on hers. For the moment I could think of nothing helpful to say.

'There is another consideration.' Armand looked grim. 'If taken and "persuaded", the boy could incriminate us all. He has been party to our own adult escapades.' He held up his hand as both Mère Poisson and I began to expostulate. 'He is but a lad. How could he stand up to those criminal bullies? I doubt whether any of us could.'

'Then what is to be done?' I picked up the fallen glass mechanically and set it on the table. 'We cannot hide Jaseur forever. There are informers in every crevice.'

Peter had been mopping up the spill. Now he put down his cloth and said in a surprisingly authoritative tone, 'There is only one thing to be done. Jaseur must come with me to England and be found a family and a trade amongst our people. I'll watch over him, you may be sure.'

'Peter! You are going home?'

'Yes. I have delayed long enough, for a reason you well know. But I can do nothing more to aid you.' He went to Mère Poisson and dropped down beside her, taking her work-worn hands in his.

'Can you give him up, *ma mère*? Will you trust me with your boy's future?'

Having seen so much grief in past months, I now felt myself to be immune to its touch. However, this mother's face was too much for me. I crept from the room and went to sit on the stoop, careless of the cold wind that turned my tears to ice on my cheeks. I knew there was no answer to life's cruelty. Mère Poisson would give up her remaining son for his sake, and Jaseur would take this opportunity. I'd miss him, but I was glad for him, although the journey to the coast and across the channel would be fraught with danger, and there were no guarantees that he, and Peter, too, would reach safety. All of life was a risk.

I pulled myself together and went back inside.

Peter had assisted Mère Poisson upstairs to talk to her son, leaving Armand to wait for me, wearing his sombre expression. I braced myself for whatever was coming.

'Juliette, did you sense any suspicion of you when you returned to the Conciergerie?' he asked.

'Why, no. I was prepared for it, but the clerk seemed to think I was Jaseur's victim, not his associate in crime.'

'Then fortune was with you. You have several times come close to disaster, and I believe it grows too dangerous to continue.'

'I cannot agree. I'm not under suspicion, and my motto has always been "Fortune favours the bold".'

He did not smile. 'There is another adage about a pitcher going too often to the well. To mix the metaphors: it only takes one misstep.'

'You are too gloomy, Armand.' An irony from one who, minutes earlier, had been snivelling on the stoop. Still, I wasn't giving up my subversive activities without good cause. And I wanted him to understand. 'Armand, I've not kept a tally of the children saved from the guillotine, but countless others have benefited from the few. You know what the money I earned has accomplished. You have seen the dozens of starving children fed and kept off the streets—'

'I watched and applauded your work. You have accomplished miracles. But it must end, Juliette. You are becoming too well known. What if your rabid friend, Maxine LeBrun, were to discover what you do? She would see only the escaped aristos, not the starving street dwellers. Do you think she would hesitate to denounce you?'

I began to feel cornered. 'There is no reason why she should learn of my activities. She's too busy with her own affairs to be interested in mine. The *Républicaines–Révolutionaires* have been forcibly disbanded. Robespierre sees them as too powerful an opposition to his will, and they are preoccupied with plotting furiously in some dark corner.'

'You avoid the issue. You are becoming too well known for your philanthropies. What if someone should question the source of the money you dispense? There are spies and informers beneath every stone. You balance on a knife-point Juliette, and never see the danger!' His voice had risen as he grew more emphatic, and I felt no desire to smile at his new mixture of metaphors. He was in total earnest.

Peter returned to the room and said, 'I heard you. What danger threatens Juliette?'

I turned to him. 'Armand is being ridiculously over-cautious—'

Armand said abruptly, 'I think you should go with Peter.'

'What?' I suddenly felt cold.

Peter said something. I heard him only vaguely. Then he shook me.

'Listen to me, Juliette. Armand is right. For weeks I have warned you of the risk if you continue these rescues. Come with Jaseur and me. In England you will be safe and can start a new life.'

A new life without Armand, I thought. How could he dismiss me so easily? We'd become so close, companions over a glass of wine, discussing all the things that had disappeared from our lives, the small pleasures that had, for a time, blotted out the bleak reality. We gave each other so much. He could not mean me to leave.

I said to Peter, 'I agree, 'tis time for you to go, Peter. You have done more than enough for a people who are not your own. Paris is descending into a pit of terror. In that, Armand is right. But I will not go with you. My place is here. Everything important to me is here. I have told you this many times.'

Peter continued to hold me, forcing me to look into his eyes. Blue as cornflowers, they were as compelling as he could make them. 'I love you, Juliette. I have from our very first meeting. My family will make you welcome and see that you have every comfort. And if … if you cannot bring yourself to return my love, will you at least accept my name and my protection? I swear to you I shall expect nothing in return.'

'Oh, Peter. Dear Peter—' I couldn't go on. To inspire such devotion was humbling, yet it also laid a huge, unwanted burden upon me.

I felt Armand's presence behind me, keeping his distance.

He said in a dispassionate tone, 'A somewhat milky declaration, but honest. You should accept the offer, Juliette.'

I swung around, pulling free of Peter's hold. 'So that's your advice, is it? To run from my responsibilities and save my own skin. How could you think so lowly of me, Armand!'

His twisted smile was an added hurt. 'I want you to live, my dear. For that, you need your skin.'

'You joke, at such a time!'

He shrugged. 'There is another benefit. You can take Clara with you. If you wed, as a family you would more easily pass the checkpoints. And of course, you would provide a home for my poor orphaned niece in England.'

I reeled. I distinctly felt the floorboards shift beneath my feet. He really meant it! It was expedient, so he'd see me wed another and go from his life without a qualm.

I couldn't take it in. Falling on to the nearest stool I covered my all-too-revealing face and struggled with my emotions.

However, Peter, impatient, soon pulled me to my feet. 'Decide now, Juliette. Will you come with me, or risk an uncertain future under a Terror that has barely begun to show its terrible strength? Will you choose life or the likelihood of a bloody death?'

I'd never heard him so serious. He was losing patience with me.

Behind me Armand laughed, scornfully, I thought. 'Persevere, Englishman. She is female, and therefore a natural ditherer.' He came close to speak in my ear, close enough for me to feel his breath on my hair. '*Nom de Dieu*, woman, listen to sense! The gutters of Paris will run with blood when Robespierre feels his full power. Guillotines are already at work all over the country, and when they cannot keep pace, there are always the barges. Oh, yes. In the south they load their victims aboard, tied together in bunches, then sink them in the river. Have you not heard what goes on? Are you unaware? Leave while you can. You have earned your life and a chance at happiness.'

Happiness! He offered me happiness a world away from him. I felt the rejection physically, as if he'd laid hands upon me and thrown me deliberately into Peter's arms. It was too much. Pain such as I'd never known welled up and spread throughout my body, from toes to fingertips and seeming to burst from the crown of my head in a fiery blaze.

I whipped around to face him, all my desperate love now revealed for him to see. But he'd turned his back, was moving away, dismissing me. I was no longer his concern.

It was like a sudden icy rain-cloud opening above my head. The fire in me died to a flicker and went out. I heard myself say in a stranger's voice, 'I will go then.'

He paused, his shoulders stiffening, then moved on. The door closed behind him.

CHAPTER 17

WHEN PETER HAD gone, weighed down by a victory that had proved hollow, I dragged myself up to my room, dreading the sleepless night ahead of me. I'd been too miserable to enter into any plans for our future together and was glad to see him go. I wanted to shut myself away, and prayed that no one would come seeking my services that night.

Mère Poisson had retired. Hearing stifled sobs coming from behind her curtain, I did not disturb her. In the far corner, however, Jaseur was sitting up, waiting for me, eager to talk of the extraordinary change in his circumstances. I don't think he'd properly realized what it meant to be cutting himself off from everything familiar. His mother would have done her best to hide her distress while enumerating all the advantages.

His eyes were starry with adventure, travel, a whole new world ahead. 'Juliette, have you heard? I'm to go to London!'

'I've heard. 'Tis a wonderful opportunity for you, Jaseur.' My smile must have been adequate, for he burbled on, never noticing my strained efforts to join in his plans.

'I'm to be put to a trade,' he announced. 'Citoyen Peter has said. And he'll watch over me and keep me from harm. But England is a wonderful place, he says. There will be other boys, and a home with good people, and a bed of my own, and food in plenty. And there'll be no "Terror". The English don't believe in it, he says.'

Peter appeared to have said quite a deal, I thought. But I did not grudge the lad his excitement, or Peter his patriotic bias. He meant to do well by Jaseur, and all praise to him. For myself, to wed the man and live beside him for the rest of my life, without love to buffer the inevitable grating of our differing personalities ... such a match would be disastrous. I was suddenly sure of it, and sure that Peter, too, must know how unsuited we were.

I sat down heavily on the side of the cot. What had I done? How could I go through with this charade of a marriage? It would end in the emotional destruction of us both. My life was here in Paris with the children. Peter and Armand were exaggerating the danger. I needed to believe this. *Ciel*! How I wanted to stay in the same city as the man I loved, just to know that he was there, to meet him, to converse, to have a relationship of some kind, however pale in comparison with my true need.

My wandering attention was caught by Armand's name. 'What did you say, Jaseur?'

'I heard Docteur Armand tell Clara how lonely he would be without her. Is Clara going somewhere, too?'

Trapped in my own mental turmoil, I could barely spare a thought for Clara's situation. Yet the word 'lonely' struck me. Was it a sop to give the child a sense of importance? 'Er ... yes. I think he wants Clara to accompany you and Peter to England.' Despite my despairing words thrown at Armand, I wasn't ready to commit to being one of the group.

Jaseur made a rude face and flung himself back on his pillow.

I said, 'I thought you liked Clara.'

'She's a baby. Me and Citoyen Peter are men, and we'll be doing men's things. I don't want to look after a baby.'

Nor did I, not just one particular child. All the children of Saint-Antoine were mine, in a way. With a jab of anger I realized that Armand had been preparing Clara for departure before discussing the proposal with anyone else. He'd been very sure of me. But he had no right. He did not control my actions. Nor did Peter, yet.

'Why are you looking cross, Juliette? I'll look after Clara if I have to.'

'I know you will, my dear.' I stood up, eager for a quiet space in which to think. 'Now you must sleep if you're to be strong enough to travel.'

As I stooped to kiss his forehead, he added, 'Don't tell Docteur Armand. I think he's very sad. He told Clara that he'd given away half his heart to her. When she asked him what he'd done with the other half, he said: "'Tis in someone else's keeping".'

In my brain, a flash of summer lightning burned a path straight through all the muddle, leaving behind a new clarity.

Armand had given away his heart to a child and to an unknown. Who else in his life might he love and lose? Another child? I think I'd have heard of it. Another woman, so well hidden that not one person had an inkling of her existence? His life was crammed to exhaustion. There was no room in it for dalliance. Which left one person: me.

He'd made it quite clear that he didn't want me and walked away, cutting off our friendship in a few words. That wasn't like Armand. Why hadn't I seen it before? He had emphasized the dangers, turned his anger upon me, then, within moments had reverted to cool dispassion – a manipulative trick that should have shown me how much he cared about the outcome. If Armand did love me, if I was the other warden of his heart, he'd have behaved exactly as he did.

How self-sacrificing was that, to ensure my safety by promoting my marriage to another man?

Yet I cautioned myself against leaping to such a conclusion. I might be deceiving myself. I might be about to make a colossal error. There was only one way to be sure, by risking humiliation and asking Armand for the truth. Whether he'd give it would depend upon my ability to break down his resolve. I must be clever, persuasive, devious if necessary. Above all, I had to make him believe in the depth of my love for him. Could I do it? Before I could reason myself out of the idea, I clapped on my hat and set off into the foggy night for Armand's lodgings in the Faubourg Saint-Martin.

At first I hurried, and not just through wariness of night prowlers. But by the time I climbed the stairs of his apartment building my feet had slowed. The enormity of what I was about to do loomed bigger than any fear. I was risking so much. I felt as though my whole life hung on the next few minutes. I reached the landing and hesitated, then raised my fist and knocked.

'Juliette! What are you doing here?' He stood back and I walked into a pleasant, fire-lit room.

I shed my coat and hat deliberately, taking time to look about me. It was very much a man's room, a handsome apartment at one time, all dark crimson from hangings to carpet, quite heavily worn. Patches on the walls showed where paintings had been removed, although a heavy bureau and chaise looked at home in their corners. Very likely they had been left as an aid to the letting of a furnished room.

I saw from the shaded lamp on the desk and the papers scattered there that Armand had been working. He was dishevelled, in his shirt-sleeves, his stock loosened, hair awry as if he'd run his fingers hastily through it. Although I stood apparently poised, words were tumbling in my head, phrases tried out and discarded, questions, accusations. I prayed that none of this was visible in my face.

Apparently it was not. Armand's surprised expression gave

way to wariness. He was expecting another round of arguments.

I plunged straight in. 'Will you miss me, Armand?'

He was pushed off balance, and for an instant I caught the flash of some strong emotion, swiftly repressed.

'Of course I'll miss you – and Jaseur, and Clara.'

'And Peter? Do you think he will make me a good husband?'

Armand stooped to lay a faggot on the fire, his face hidden as he replied, 'He seems a decent man.'

'But is that the only quality upon which to base a marriage? Is it decency I should look for as he takes me in his arms on our wedding night? Can I not aspire to passion, to the drumbeat in the blood, to desire and need and fulfilment?' So, what had happened to the clever phrase, the delicate extraction of information? Gone. Lost in the uprush of emotion that swept through me at the very sight of this man.

Armand's back was to me as he rested his arms on the mantel and gazed into the flames beneath. He sounded hoarse. 'I cannot say. These things will surely follow if ... when ... you are better acquainted.'

I laughed. 'We have been well acquainted these twelve months. I am fond of Peter, but I do not love him. My pulse does not throb when he enters the room. I do not listen for his footsteps in the street or strive to control the blood flushing my cheeks when he speaks to me. My thoughts are not with him while I work; and at night my dreams of ecstasy are not centred upon him as my lover and my partner in life.'

'Stop it, Juliette!'

'Why? Can you not advise me, as a friend? You are my friend?'

'I— Yes, I am your friend. But these matters are not to be discussed between friends. They are intimate—'

'And you have no wish to be intimate with me, Armand?'

He swung around sharply. *'Pour l'amour de Dieu*, Juliette!'

My heart seemed to swell in my breast as I recognized the torment he could not hide. His pallor, the set of his jaw and, beyond all else, the fire in those amazing eyes gave him away.

'Armand, you must answer me honestly. Do you send me away as a concerned friend, or because you love me enough to send me to another man to save my life?'

I thought he'd give me *some* answer. I thought – I don't know what I thought, beyond a desperate hope that he would be sufficiently shaken to speak the truth.

But as the seconds dragged out and he neither moved nor answered, just appeared to gaze through me, I grew nervous. Had I misjudged after all? Could I have revealed myself in all my emotional nakedness, embarrassed us both, and all for nothing? Was he even now trying to frame an answer that would leave me some small shred of dignity?

At last I could stand it no longer. Snatching up my coat I ran from the room. I was beyond humiliation, beyond caring about anything but the awful realization that I'd gambled my chance of happiness and lost.

Lovers are such fools – blindly throwing the dice and opening themselves to the vagaries of fate. But what is life without love, without the tremendous risk of surrendering one's heart and hopes to another human being? Every second of life is a risk. The pond newt in the rapture of mating may fall unknowing into the frog's waiting mouth; a man may be struck down at the very moment of success; and love might turn to hatred, or worse, to ennui.

Yet lovers discount any risk. And Armand and I – oh how we loved!

For he came after me. I'd just reached the head of the stairs when he called to me to wait. I teetered there, overbalanced, and found myself clutched and held to him with the fervour of a drowning man seizing a rescuer. I was squeezed half to death and gasping for air.

'How did you know, Juliette?'

I waited until my brain stopped spinning and looked up at him. His face was alight, but was it joy or despair that had finally cracked his composure? 'You have just demonstrated it most forcibly, Armand,' I replied.

His grip tightened. Did this mean he would not let me go? In my mind I willed it to be so. He must want me to stay. He must.

I had my answer when his mouth came down hard on mine.

We stood locked together in a timeless space, at length to draw apart and gaze at each other in wonder.

'I'd no idea—' I began.

'How strange—' he said.

'Why "strange", Armand?'

He ran his hand over my hair and rested it at my nape. 'Strange that I have never before known such a joyful sense of completion. I have loved before, or thought I loved. But 'twas not like this … I did not know—'

I hugged my delight in silence. There would be another time to speak of his marriage and the woman who had damaged him. This was my moment.

Cupping his dear face I said, 'You were foolish to try to deceive me, my love. You hurt me deeply. But I forgive you.'

'Indeed, milady? Shall I enumerate all the things I have forgiven you in the space of our acquaintance? You have lied to me, broken the law, embarrassed me before my peers and deceived me times without number. Yet *you* can forgive *me*!'

I agreed, happily, and kissed him. From there, one thing led on to another, and I soon found myself unclothed, in bed, and unashamedly ready to give myself to this man.

I'd dreamed of ecstasy and had never known its power and

perfection. Held, enfolded and desiring, I felt his breath mingle with mine. Each caress was an affirmation, each touch of his lips a sealing of our pact to be as one, for all time. I gloried in his golden gaze, felt my bones soften in the heat of our loving.

He lay above me and whispered words that are mine alone to remember, his fingers trailing the length of my throat, his mouth following. I twined myself about his body and shivered at the friction of skin on skin. I kissed his eyelids and wept tears of joy. My fingers skimmed and paused, feeling, knowing, taking possession, even in the moment of surrender.

And finally I slept, my head on his shoulder, his arm about me, secure, and utterly fulfilled.

CHAPTER 18

O F COURSE, THERE was now no question of my leaving. As Armand said, he could not do without me, come the Terror, come the Holocaust. He admitted his selfishness, then took me in his arms and proceeded to demonstrate once more his need for me. We were both bound up in our mutual obsession and not prepared to count the possible cost in the future.

At last I sat up and reached for my garments. 'I must tell Peter, immediately,' I said. 'I have taken advantage of him, and 'tis not kind.'

Armand drew me down beside him. 'Indeed. But another hour will not matter.'

I sat up again. 'What of Clara? I cannot ask Peter to take on responsibility for a little girl as well as Jaseur.'

Armand nibbled my ear, sending a delightful shiver down my spine. He said, 'My darling, Clara is my responsibility and she should remain with me. Will you wed me and my encumbrance?'

'Encumbrance! How can you so miscall the dearest child—'

His teasing smile silenced me. 'You are already a favourite with Clara. And with me, in case it has escaped your notice. *Eh bien*! Will you, or will you not be my bride?'

I gave him what I hoped was a most satisfactory answer.

We went together to tell Peter of the change in plans. He was naturally unhappy about my decision, yet he understood. Apparently he'd known that Armand was my choice long before I knew myself, and was now resigned to it. He managed to greet Armand amicably and upon common ground: the agreement that I should give up my 'dangerous' activities as a stealer of proscribed children. I was not consulted.

In a haze of love, which definitely affects the will, I listened to the two of them arrange my affairs, nodded and said nothing, while privately reserving the right to make my own decisions. There would be battles ahead, but not just yet. I wanted a little time to be happy before the outside world forced itself upon me.

While preparations went ahead for Peter's and Jaseur's departure, I avoided Maxine, whose jubilance over the Queen's death was hard to endure. Her behaviour became daily more offensive and, as I no longer believed in the Revolution, we had nothing left in common. The mass execution of the Girondins was another blow, followed by the worst yet.

This was a note delivered by the grubby hand of a street child. Heaven alone knew what twisted pathway it travelled before it reached me. Camille had written me a farewell. Claude de Cassonnière had been guillotined and she and little Jean-Claude had been thrown into the Temple prison, a fortress I could not hope to penetrate. Their execution would inevitably follow within a matter of weeks.

Armand tried to alleviate my distress with a practical suggestion. 'Wait until they are moved to the Conciergerie, as they will be, prior to judgement and execution. Then they will come within your reach.'

His unspoken acceptance of the risk warmed me. He understood how important it was for me to rescue my dear Camille and her child. Yet I feared that I'd fail.

I said, 'I've already thought of every possible scheme, and several impossible ones. My mind feels hollow and useless.

Perhaps I could spirit out Jean-Claude in the false bottomed coffin scheme, but not a healthy young woman like Camille. For some reason, the guard is much heavier now. Perhaps those in charge have reviewed the false alarm over the Queen. Everyone going in or out is scrutinized. And the episode of Jaseur's theft has damaged my standing, although I am not yet suspect.'

I could not give up and, with Armand's help, I continued to plot ways and means, but with the heart taken out of me. The situation had gone on for so long, with such effort put in for so little reward. Yes, I'd rescued a number of children from the guillotine, and even more from starvation, temporarily. Still, I failed to think of a stratagem that would save Camille and my little godchild.

My gift of joy had been swamped by another desperate struggle, and not even Armand's loving concern could help.

The weather turned bitter as the once-celebrated Christmas season approached. I was called out to a sick woman whose family had tried the traditional treatment for pleurisy without success, and was now reduced to my less bizarre treatments. The poor woman had suffered some twenty hours of attachment to a rotting pigeon split down the back while alive and still warm when applied to her chest. My sympathies were also with the pigeon. But by the time I left, having forbidden the use of further livestock, as well as grandmama's mustard and urine poultice, I could be reasonably certain that the patient would recover.

On the way home, by chance I met Maxine in the street. Her draggled appearance showed her deterioration and she was clearly the worse for drink. She grasped my arm and announced that I must go with her to take part in the new celebration designed by the heads of the Paris Sections.

'What celebration? I don't have the time, Maxine—'

She insisted, overriding my protests and dragging me along with her in the direction of the river. She was as raucous as a bargee fresh from a tavern spree. '*Parbleu*! Paris has seen nothing like it. 'Tis to be a Festival of Reason held in the old cathedral. You must join us.'

I resisted, digging in my heels and skating uselessly on the cobbles. 'Stop. I cannot go with you, Maxine.'

'Why not?' She turned on me, her face creased with suspicion. 'You never join in our celebrations. You keep to yourself, like some fancy bourgeoise. Do you hold up your nose at us low *sans-culottes*, eh? Is that it?'

I shrugged. 'No. Why should you think so? I am simply too busy.'

'*Tiens*! Not too busy for a day like this one,' she countered, and proceeded to tow me away like a river barge.

I adopted an eager expression and submitted. She was dangerous in her present mood and, with all that was presently going on in my life, I couldn't afford to arouse her inquisitiveness. She had the instincts of a terrier smelling out rats.

The sights and sounds of the monstrous 'festival' performed in the hallowed precincts of Notre Dame are buried at the back of my mind. I hope never again to see such desecration and debauchery as I did that day. At the height of the proceedings, almost submerged in a tide of half-naked men and women all stamping and howling the Revolutionary '*Ça Ira*' as the Goddess of Reason was enthroned on the altar and adored by her copulating devotees, I fled. Careless of Maxine's reaction, I fought my way out and ran all the way back to Rue Bitone, to the sanity of Mère Poisson's kitchen and the everyday lives of normal people.

But I knew I'd made an enemy. When she'd recovered from her excesses, Maxine would remember my horrified response to her festival, and mark it against me.

We saw Peter and Jaseur off one day early in the New Year. They were dressed as peasants supposedly returning home from market, and smelled all too realistically of manure. Armand shook hands with Peter, grinning as he said, 'Remember your disguise. Do not emulate the late Chevalier de Vallonce, who, when escaping dressed as a poor shoe mender, absently ordered an extravagant meal at an inn.' He then turned aside as Peter took me in his arms and we exchanged the first and last kiss of our relationship.

'We shall not meet again,' he said, his cheek pressed hard against mine.

'Perhaps, one day, when all this is over.' I could hear the denial in my voice. 'Peter, I will always remember you as the truest of friends. Thank you for all your help and support.'

He abruptly released me and faced Armand, saying, 'You have been given a treasure. See that you guard her well.' Picking up his pack, he left the room.

I turned to Jaseur with tears in my eyes and tucked my best woollen scarf around his neck. 'Be careful, and obey Peter instantly. You will be in danger until you reach England.' I hugged him and stepped back, letting his mother enfold him for the last time. Armand and I exchanged glances and went to wait outside with Peter.

We accompanied the travellers as far as the end of the rue Saint-Antoine. The Porte Royale was the safest gate, facing eastwards and away from the coast. It was assumed that escapees would prefer to start from north or west. We scarce dared breathe while the two presented their forged travel documents. Yet all went well, and without a backward look they passed out of our lives.

I'd resumed my work as medical attendant to the inmates of the Conciergerie, although abandoning any attempt to liberate more children. The tightened controls were strictly maintained and the difficulties in the way of a rescue seemed insuperable.

Nonetheless, on the day that Camille and Jean-Claude were transferred from the Temple to the 'Anteroom to Hell', I knew I would make one more attempt.

''Tis madness! You cannot take the risk!' Armand had lost control, his good intentions forgotten. He stormed about his room, sending papers flying from his desk, jingling china on the shelf. The shabby carpet rucked under his feet and dust flew up as I stood and let the tempest rage about me.

I'd expected this reaction. It was natural. But I could not let him break my resolve. Camille and her child were my family. They were all I loved, apart from Armand himself, and I could not weigh them against one another. Whatever happened, Armand would be safe. My life was still my own to risk.

Armand halted in front of me. 'What madcap plan do you have in mind? Whatever it is, I intend to be a part of it.'

'No, Armand. This is my responsibility.'

'Nonsense! Whatever affects you, affects me. We are as much wed as if we'd stood before a priest – and one day we shall find one who will say the words over us.'

Our gazes locked. I said, 'I must do this alone. My plan cannot include anyone else.'

For a long moment those blazing eyes held me, seeming to penetrate my brain, examining every thought, every feeling. Then I was released. Armand threw himself into a chair, saying, 'Tell me your plan. Perhaps it could benefit from another viewpoint.'

The following day I visited the women's yard and sought out Camille's cell. It was bitterly cold, with snow lying thick on the paving, and not much warmer inside. My breath hung in the air before me, like some evil miasma. Even my teeth ached with the cold.

I had expected a change in Camille, but I was appalled at her appearance. Sunken-faced, her gown hanging like a sheet from thin shoulder bones, she was a shadow, a ghost of the beautiful young woman I'd known.

'What have they done to you, Camille!' Ghostly words from the past, spoken on that day when I'd discovered her in labour and close to death.

She said in an expressionless voice, 'Why did you come? You should not have come.'

I tried to hide my dismay. 'I came because you need help. I am going to get you and Jean-Claude out of here.'

She repeated, 'You should not have come. There is no way out save by the guillotine's blade. Go away, Juliette.'

I took the fishbone fingers in mine and drew her to a seat on the palliasse that was her bed. Jean-Claude lay asleep on the floor, his couch a heap of rags. He, too, had the grey pallor of weeks in prison and precious little food, by the look of him. He snuffled and coughed in his sleep, and I heard the air wheezing in his chest.

Shaken with anger and pity, I steadied myself before speaking. 'There *is* a way out, Camille, if you are brave. 'Tis a risk, I admit. Yet we must try, if only for Jean-Claude's sake.'

Her dulled eyes went to the sleeping child and I saw a momentary flicker.

I pressed her. 'You must think of him. Come, let me explain my plan.'

I finally left the chilly cell in a disturbed frame of mind. I could not congratulate myself upon my success. Camille seemed strangely inert. Of course, I'd no way of knowing what she had suffered in the Temple prison. There was a lingering terror behind her calm. It showed in her nervous start when someone spoke from behind her, and in her ceaseless watching over Jean-Claude. But she would not speak of it. Of course, she would also be grieving for her dead husband. Still, I hoped to gain her support, eventually.

My plan initially involved Jean-Claude. However, I was hesitant to drug a child whose breathing was already badly affected. I needed to find another way. As for Camille, she appeared so wayward, so little in charge of herself that I couldn't depend upon her remembering any instructions, let alone following them swiftly and faithfully.

I felt close to despair. I'd reached the point of accepting possible failure. And envisaging Camille's lonely trip to the guillotine, I knew that I could not let her die without one caring person there. It would take all the strength I possessed, but I'd do it, if I had to. But I would not have to! Where was my courage and inventiveness? There would be a way. I just needed to work harder at finding it.

I spent the whole night trying to rearrange my escape plan, without much success. The next day, when Armand saw me, he insisted upon doing my round at the prison while I snatched a little sleep. He pointed out that I was in no state to persuade a kitten to drink milk, let alone a terrified and exhausted woman to plot an escape. I was forced to agree.

I still occupied my rooms with Mère Poisson, who was failing rapidly and needed some supervision. She missed Jaseur badly, and I tried to spend time with her to help fill the empty hours. My sallies into the world dressed as a woman had almost ceased through lack of time, lack of desire for even the enjoyment of a glass of wine in a café, and the increasing danger in the streets. A woman without the distinctive regalia of a *Révolutionnaire* was inviting trouble, while a woman in tricolour dress would be swept up into the hazardous activities of her rampaging 'sisters'.

Armand's report that evening was disturbing. He placed a hand on my shoulder and pressed me into a chair before saying, 'I believe your Camille's mind has been affected by her sufferings. And her child is seriously ill.'

Mère Poisson's fire was a comfort. I turned my face to its warmth, saying, 'I was afraid of that. I mean, afraid that Jean-Claude's lungs were affected. But Camille—'

'Is beyond help. You can place no dependence upon her co-operation in an escape attempt.'

I let my head fall in my hands. 'What am I to do? How can I hope to get them out?'

'I do not believe that she wishes to escape. Juliette, you cannot force someone to want to go on living.'

I sat up. 'I can and I will. Camille is worn down, but if she is given hope of a new life for herself and Jean-Claude, surely she will revive.'

'Look at me, Juliette.'

I did, reluctantly, and saw the pity in his face.

'Learn to let go, *ma mie*. Some things in this world are simply not possible.'

'No! I will not give up. We meet again tomorrow, and you know I can be very persuasive.'

'I know.' His smile could not hide his belief that this time I'd fail.

That night I could not sleep at all. I ached, physically and mentally, my whole being in turmoil as I acknowledged that Armand was only saying what I'd refused to admit. As the consequence of failure rose before my mind's eye in hideous detail, my anguish became an acid rising in my throat, corroding my mouth as I vomited until I could barely stand. Exhausted, I lay on my bed and pictured this friend of a lifetime who meant so much to me. I could not bear to lose her, or the babe who was everything to her. I would make one last attempt to show Camille that she must help me to help her.

I left early for the Conciergerie, not wanting to meet my prag-matic love and have him undermine my determination. He still kept his room across the city and occupied it on at least one night of the week. Last night he'd returned there, called back urgently to a particular patient. But I knew he would return early, to be at hand if I needed him.

There was some kind of confusion in the female yard. I fought my way through a group of murmuring women clustered about Camille's cell.

I think I knew I'd find tragedy there. When I entered, Camille lay on her straw bedding, crooning to the child in her arms. Two women stood before her, arms akimbo, looking fiercely protective, while those outside were pressing in, their murmurs growing into accusations.

I looked down at Jean-Claude's still form. 'What has happened?'

One of the protectors met my gaze with defiance. 'She killed him, smothered him in his sleep. I would do the same myself, rather than see his head struck off.'

I'd witnessed such scenes before, all too often. Sadly, I felt the child's neck, just to be sure. There was no pulse. He was stiff and cold, a lifeless mannikin. When I tried to release him from Camille's clutch, she screamed and held him close. Her eyes were wild as she scrambled to huddle in the corner. She didn't seem to know me.

'Her mind has gone,' said someone, and the accusing voices stilled.

''Tis little wonder,' said another. 'I heard what they did to her in the Temple.'

I knelt down to allow Camille to examine my face. And as her eyes travelled over me, the madness cleared, bringing recognition.

She said, 'He is with God and the angels. They will care for him.'

'Camille—' My voice stuck in my throat.

Her smile was a travesty. 'You do not have to find words,

Juliette. I know what I am. I know that I must atone for my dreadful deed. Hell's fires await me.'

'God will understand.' I heard myself with disbelief, I, who had no religion beyond my calling!

Dry wisps of hair, streaked with grey, fell loose as she shook her head. 'There can be no forgiveness. But of your charity, pray for me as I go to the scaffold. Perhaps He will hear *your* voice.'

I scanned the faces crowding about us, some still hostile, others grieving with the forlorn woman on the straw. This was no time to be talking of escape plots. I said, 'Give him to me, Camille. He's mine, too. I will give him Christian burial.'

She barely hesitated. 'Here then. Take him.' With a last kiss on his cold cheek, she handed Jean-Claude's body to me. 'Do not come again, Juliette. This is our final farewell.'

'You cannot mean that—'

'My name is listed for the morning.' Her tone had a dreadful finality.

'Dear God!' I fell back on my heels, speechless.

Again she smiled, this time with a little of the old warmth. 'You cannot know how glad I am to be leaving this life, Juliette. But it grieves me to leave you. You have been the dearest friend to me.'

At last I found my voice. 'And you to me. I would have given years of my life to save you and little Jean-Claude.'

'No one could have saved us. We were meant to die, along with so many other victims of this vile regime.' She sighed. 'Go now. I must be at my prayers. I have only tonight to beg the Holy Mother's intercedence for another mother in dreadful need.'

I rose unsteadily, still holding close the dead child. Bending, I kissed Camille, feeling her frail clasp about my shoulders. 'God be with you, dear Camille. I promise to be there when you … when you go. Look for me.'

She held me a moment, then let her arms fall. Blinded by tears, I turned and blundered past the crowding women, out into the cold yard.

CHAPTER 19

A S I'D PROMISED Camille, we buried little Jean-Claude in the corner of a graveyard, secretly, and said our own prayers over the pathetic mound of soil. If there was a priest left in Paris who had not turned his coat, we did not know of him; and nothing could have been more heartfelt than my petition for the little soul's rest. I still harboured doubts about its efficacy, but I had to try.

Armand had made a tiny coffin from a cupboard shelf and I sacrificed a shift in which to wrap the child, weeping as I did so, the more because Camille was not there to do it. We had no flowers with which to deck the grave. In any case, these could have drawn attention to it. So Armand stamped down the soil and covered this with a slab of fallen marble. Then we crept away like thieves through the forest of broken columns and other ornamental edifices to the dead.

By day, the Terror was overwhelming. Spies haunted the alleys and arcades, eavesdropping in the long bread lines, leaving people afraid to exchange a word on the street. There was forced conscription, requisitioning, open plunder and murder, all done in the name of the Republic. Men were forced into the new workshops erected in the gardens of the Tuileries. There they manufactured muskets and cannon from metal melted down from church bells, altars and objects confiscated from houses abandoned by *émigrés*. Everyone watched everyone else. No one was safe.

On the morning of Camille's execution I rose early. Dressed in my male attire, for safety, I hurried to find a position in the Place de la Révolution where I could watch her arrive. I'd told Armand that I wanted to do this alone. Perhaps it was my guilt at being a survivor. Perhaps it was the thought that this was just between Camille and me, reflecting our years-long friendship.

I secured a position near the scaffold and tried not to listen to the comments from the crowd. A cold, lifeless sun had cleared the rooftops by the time I heard the tumbrels' rumbling, followed a moment later by a roar of excitement that rose into the chill air. People never seemed to tire of the spectacle of public execution, named by one of the deputies as 'the red Mass', and the guillotine as its 'great altar'. They brought their children and purchased wine and food from hawkers as they waited for the performance to begin. Nearby, the notorious tricoteuses grouped themselves around the scaffold, chatting away like witches on holiday.

Icicles hung from eaves, dripping down the necks of people crowding close. My face stung with the cold and my exhaled breath clouded around me like smoke. Yet, I could not escape the overpowering stench of unwashed human beings, half-frozen filth in the kennels, and above all, the charnel house reek of blood-soaked straw left over from the previous day.

I'd prepared myself to wait through any number of executions until Camille's turn arrived. But as the first cart appeared, surrounded by guardsmen, I saw her standing at the front like a proud figurehead. Her hair had been hacked off and her hands bound behind her, yet she held herself erect as she swayed with the jolting movement. She scanned the crowd and I thrust forward, willing her to see me.

Our eyes met and she smiled. It was the old Camille standing there, bravely facing her fate.

They say that, with death imminent, images of one's early life flash through the mind. I don't know whether it was so for Camille. For me, at that moment, the crowd, the scaffold, everything around faded and I was a child again on a summer's afternoon, playing in the stream beyond the château walls. Camille stood beside me, bare-legged, her skirts kilted up, laughing as I splashed her with mud from the dam walls we were constructing.

I heard her say: 'There's a great hole in your dyke. The fish will escape, silly.'

And the scene slipped away as drums began to beat, heralding a new parade of death.

A strange numbness crept over me as I watched the prisoners dragged from the carts and marshalled for their last short walk upon this earth. The first in line, an elderly man, had to be helped up the steps to the platform. He stood with blind eyes raised to the sky, his nearly-bald head caught and haloed by a ray of sunlight. Then he was thrown on to the board, bound, and slid forward. The drumming ceased and the blade dropped. So did his head. Blood gushed over the executioner, who cursed as he stepped back. The crowd cheered. And it was over. Just like that. A life snuffed out with no more thought than the pinching of a candle wick.

A woman sidled up and poked me in the ribs. I turned to see a raddled face grinning drunkenly, the eyes as dead as last week's fish. Her voice was similarly lifeless as she invited me in the crudest terms to enjoy sexual congress with her at the cost of a few sous.

My expression was enough to have her slink off in search of other prey.

While I waited, two more men were despatched, one entertaining the watchers with a ribald speech that was cut off mid-sentence. The stench of fresh blood grew.

Then Camille was brought forward.

The crowd drew in its collective breath, titillated by the sight of a beautiful woman facing death. For she was beautiful. The greyness that I'd seen in her had disappeared, as a rain cloud passes from the sun. Her blue eyes, lucid as crystal, gazed into mine, sending a message of love and fearlessness that lifted my heavy heart. Camille had made her peace with God, after all.

She mounted the slippery steps and stood for a moment with her face raised, eyes closed, clearly praying. Then, as the drums began their beat, she was grasped and flung on to the board. She turned her head towards me, mouthing the words 'Jean-Claude'. I nodded and clasped my hands in prayer position. Again she smiled.

I heard the rattle of the blade being raised, saw the board slide forward, heard the thump of the neck clamp. With bile in my throat, I watched the blade fall, then I turned and forced my way through the crowd.

My foot slipped in a pool of blood and a dog ran to lick it up. Someone kicked it away, laughing. It seemed the whole world was tainted with that coppery scent. Sick with grief and impotent rage, I remembered the day that I'd entered Paris and had seen blood flowing in the gutter. And still it flowed in a seemingly endless stream. When would it end? When would the scarlet, blood-soaked wind that raged throughout France die away and let the survivors try to renew whatever remained of our once proud land?

Suddenly I could bear it no longer. I turned my face to the nearest wall and cried bitterly, pounding my fists upon the stones, welcoming the pain – anything to dull the unbearable agony of despair.

I felt arms enfold me. Armand. With my head resting on his

shoulder, I heard him murmur that we must leave this place, that I should never have come alone. I clung to him briefly, then let him lead me away.

We crossed the river and walked for a long time in silence. Armand sensed my need for a quiet period in which to regain my emotional balance. I'd known the day would be hard, and it was, unbelievably traumatic. Yet, with the death of Camille I had a sense of settlement, of an inevitable conclusion. France was ridding herself of one whole sector of society, and for those who escaped the guillotine, life would never again be as they remembered it.

Camille was a member of the nobility, an aristocrat of the bluest blood. To live at the level of the bourgeoisie would have been a misery for her. She had lost everything that she prized – home, position, husband and child – and been imprisoned and degraded in ways I could only imagine. Finally, she'd been driven to madness and murder. Yet, somehow this courageous woman had pulled herself back, had reconciled the Church's teachings with her God, and was at peace when she died.

For that reason I would no longer weep for her. My tears would be selfish ones for my own loss.

The gardens of the old Luxembourg Palace were winter-bound and colourless. Still, it soothed me to wander the gravelled walks between the dormant garden beds, with Armand keeping pace beside me. It seemed that we communicated on another level, without the need of speech. I was aware of his loving concern and his acceptance of my wish to do things my way. He had followed me to the Place de la Révolution, but waited until I needed him before approaching. While I was in utter distress he willingly took charge. When I had recovered, he allowed me to set the pace, to choose to be silent, to use him as I pleased. That was the measure of his love.

*

By the end of 1794, we knew the Revolution was approaching crisis point. Armand grew increasingly agitated as he saw Robespierre and his Jacobin cohorts increase their grip on the Committee of Public Safety to the point where no one dared oppose them. No one but George Danton.

'But a different George Danton,' Armand told me as we walked home from the Conciergerie. He had taken to meeting me after my work day finished, and accompanying me on the long walk home.

'How is he different?'

'Since those weeks spent away from Paris on his farm he has grown softer. He is more interested in saving lives and stopping all this senseless killing.'

'Well, that surely is a change to the good.'

Armand shook his head. 'He is going against serious adversaries, like Hébert with his mad-dog followers, and Robespierre, who daily grows in importance.' He paused in the middle of the bridge and leaned upon the balustrade.

I joined him, gazing down at the muddy flow of the Seine. For me, George Danton's problems still evoked little interest, despite his more recent efforts to halt the excesses of the Revolution. However, he was Armand's friend and thus deserving of my consideration.

Two days later we were again returning from the Conciergerie when the man himself appeared, marching across the road from the Tuileries and hailing Armand as he approached.

'George!' Armand grasped his friend's hand. 'What news?'

'Very bad, I'm afraid.' He shook his leonine head. 'Can we go somewhere and talk? I need to clear my mind, and my mouth is as dry as a kiln.'

We exchanged a brief greeting. However, my attempt to go on alone was thwarted by Armand, who insisted we three repair to a wineshop. He had no intention of letting me walk home by myself. I appreciated his concern for my safety, and of course I enjoyed his company. So I resigned myself. Wine would warm me from the inside on this cold evening, and I need not participate in what would clearly be a political discussion. However, despite my unwillingness, it took only a few minutes before I found myself drawn in. Armand was right: Danton had changed.

Once ensconced in the wineshop of his choice, a dingy room smelling of wine lees and dust, he slumped in his chair and waited to be served. He was apparently in no rush to speak.

When he finally did, it seemed to me that some of the old magnetism had faded, dulling his tone. 'We are descending into madness, you know. The Revolutionary Tribunal is charging people on the words of vindictive neighbours and children. I heard today of one woman, wrongly gaoled through confusion over another prisoner with a similar name. The prosecutor simply said: "Since she's here, we might just as well take her." And he signed the death warrant! Recently, in Lyons, Fouché thought the guillotine was too slow a method of execution and had more than three hundred mown down by cannon fire.' He heaved a great sigh. 'What have we become? What manner of distorted beings are we, that we allow such happenings in the name of patriotism?'

I sat dumb, appalled, while Armand gazed at his friend and waited. When Danton held the floor, few tried to interrupt.

He sat silent for a time, his thick fingers playing with the stem of his glass, twisting it back and forth while he gazed broodingly into the ruby depths.

Eventually he said, 'Had I not retired from the Committee of Public Safety last year and let Robespierre take over, the

Girondins would not have been overthrown. I could have fought to save the Queen and win some accord with the enemies at our borders. But I was weary. I needed to go home to Arcis and lie fallow for a while. God forgive me for my selfishness.' He tossed down his wine and waited for the glass to be refilled before continuing.

'I dreamed of a great Republic that all the world would envy. Instead, Robespierre has let killers and sadists have full rein, while I played at farming and "rested". I should have known there was no time for men of good will to rest.'

Armand's brows rose. 'You know he hates you and suspects that you mock him in the privacy of your circle of friends.'

'What of it?' Danton flicked his fingers in a derogatory sign. 'The man is a eunuch. His vital juices are channelled into work and more work – the reshaping of France according to his plan. But he has gone about it the wrong way. He has unleashed a monster that will eventually turn on him and destroy him, along with his cold, intellectual dreams. I have just told him so.'

'You saw him?'

Danton looked grim. 'He all but had me thrown down the stairs. I can no longer talk with the creature.' He thumped down his glass and rose.

Armand stood as well. 'Why do you leave? We've scarce begun to talk.'

'I have cleared my mind and my throat, and must be away. Forgive me for delaying you.' He bowed in my direction. 'Your servant, *Citoyen Docteur*.'

'George! You cannot just go—' Armand's surprise was edged with anger.

But George had gone.

I said to Armand, 'For a large man, he can move like genie. Here one minute, gone the next.'

'For a man with a large brain, he is being exceedingly dense.

Robespierre is his deadly enemy, and George has been too long away to realize the extent of his megalomania. He will bring George down if he can.'

I shivered. 'Those things he said about the killings ... so much evil in the hearts of men ... and women.'

'Yes. I fear we have not yet seen the worst.' Armand drained his glass and set it down. 'We may as well leave, too. Unless you would like more wine?'

I said wearily, 'Like Danton, I am weary. So very weary. Let us go home.'

But I was more than weary. Something weighed on my spirits that was stronger than sorrow, deeper than exhaustion. As we walked the narrow, darkened streets of Saint-Antoine I felt a prickling along my spine that sent alarm signals through every nerve. I peered anxiously into each alley and doorway, as fearful as a rabbit scenting the dogs. I longed to dive into my own burrow, to be safe from the night. It was an entirely animal fear that gripped me, basic and undeniable. I'd never felt this way before, as an overwhelming dread threatened to send me fleeing into the dark.

Armand sensed something, and he grasped my arm. 'You tremble, Juliette! What is it?'

'I—' My throat had closed. Swallowing, I spoke in panicked jerks. 'I am possessed ... by terror ... for no ... reason.'

'Did you hear something? See something?' His gaze darted about, scanning the dark chasm created by the buildings. There were no street lamps in the Saint-Antoine, and tonight a pale sickle moon had sunk below the rooftops, while the swatch of stars trapped between overhanging eaves were as useless as glow-worms in a cavern.

With his hand on me, my trembling steadied. I remembered that I was not alone. ''Tis leaving,' I said.

'What do you mean?'

'The fear is fading away.' I gave a deep sigh, releasing the tension. 'I feel foolish. I cannot even say what it was I feared. I just panicked, I suppose because I am weary beyond belief. Forgive me for being so nonsensical, Armand.'

He did not answer immediately. Finally he said, 'I cannot dismiss it so lightly. Such an experience might come from the very depths of the self. Perhaps something, at some level of perception, is warning you to take care.'

'Armand!'

He began to hurry me along. 'We can discuss this later. Now we should get off the street, quickly.'

CHAPTER 20

THE HEAT BEGAN to build early that spring, presaging a fierce summer to come, and Armand took this as an excuse to coax me into moving to his apartment.

''Tis much cooler with the high ceilings, and I can clear a space for you to conduct your medical examinations. Clara would welcome your company as, of course, would I.'

Since we were at the time lying amongst his bed pillows and his suggestion was accompanied by a most seductive stroking of my neck and shoulders, I had no trouble believing him.

'You would be even closer to the Conciergerie, and might return here earlier each day,' he added. His insinuating tone made me blush. I laughed but, against my own inclination, I still resisted.

'No, Armand. My people need to know where to find me. They trust me to come when I'm needed, especially the children.' I moved away from that provocative hand and rose from the tangled sheets. 'If the heat beneath the roof becomes impossible to bear, I shall find a street-front room near Mère Poisson's house. There is always one at a price.' Thanks to Armand's generosity, and his paying patients, that price could be met.

Armand gave way without argument. It was another instance of his willingness to accord me equality and the right to pursue my own path. We had achieved a rare balance in our relationship and I took care to maintain such a precious state. Of course, he took a harder line if he foresaw danger or real difficulties ahead. That was only male protectiveness and, as a female, I preened, even while maintaining my position.

To own the truth, I had been leading a deliberately circumspect life since that night when, walking home with Armand, a sudden unexplainable fear had nearly paralysed me. These days I made sure to wear the tricolour cockade in my hat, and looked scruffier than I liked in an unironed shirt and a badly fitting coat. I did my work at the prison and left before dusk. Back at the Rue Bitone I saw those of my patients who would come to me, and ventured out at night only if called urgently. The residue of that crippling fear had stayed with me and, for the first time in my life, I felt the need to protect myself.

I did wonder whether the dread I felt was an intimation of danger threatening Armand, whom I loved more than life. I had no reason to think so, and yet that worry lay at the back of my mind.

In the meantime, fate was rushing upon George Danton. His rousing declaration in the Convention that the Terror had once served a useful purpose, but it should not hurt innocent people, had been greeted with the enthusiasm reserved for an ice-water douche in winter. His further insistence that the time had come to be sparing of human blood brought down a torrent of rage from the Jacobins. A mighty struggle was taking place between the advocates of clemency and the adherents of the Terror, and no one could guess who would be the winners.

I'd managed to avoid Maxine since our last unfortunate meeting, but it was inevitable that we should come across one another again. It happened at one of the ghastly community functions known at the Fraternal Suppers. At these weekly gatherings, neighbours were expected to provide a contribution of food and sit down at a communal board and demonstrate how much they were enjoying each other's company – or suffer the consequences. These horrible travesties could not be avoided, and one day late in March I found myself on a bench in the street, squeezed between a known *tricoteuse* and a terrified laundry maid. Facing me from the opposite bench was Maxine. Half of Paris was falling down drunk, mostly in an effort to quell fear, and Maxine was no exception. But her first words, uttered in a sneering tone, alerted me to danger.

'*Hé*, little *Docteur*. Not in your petticoats today? Too busy strutting in the prison yards and puffing off your importance, I suppose.' She wagged a dirty finger in my face.

Fortunately, no one seemed interested. The crone next to me mumbled assiduously over a chicken bone and my other neighbours, too, were picking at the food like a jostling of hungry crows.

'*Bonjour*, Maxine,' I said. 'How goes it with you?' It took an effort to be pleasant, when clearly she intended to annoy. I passed her an appetizing dish of eels and forced a smile.

Ignoring the eels, she leaned forward into my face. A gust of foul breath laced with brandy hit me and I couldn't help flinching.

Of course, she took it amiss. 'Oh, aren't we dainty today? What do the likes of you care how I fare? What do any of you care?' She belched and looked around her fiercely. 'You're all afraid for yourselves. Every one of you hides behind the door, afraid to be on the streets like a good patriot should be, smelling the … smelling out the treacherous rats, the stinking traitors—' Her voice died away and she sat, glassy eyed, as if communing with herself.

She looked dreadful, a greasy-haired slattern whose clothes were falling apart and whose person had not seen soap and water for days, perhaps weeks. I wondered what had happened to bring her to such a pass. Brandy, certainly. But it occurred to me that other forms of excess could act upon a person's nature and bring on a form of mania. Surely her continual ranting and rampaging about the streets, the physical violence in which she habitually indulged, the total lack of restraint of any kind, must have a harmful effect. The gleam in her once lovely eyes as she looked up at me was definitely not sane.

'I liked you,' she muttered. 'You were one of the brave ones. You believed in women's rights … you bit your thumb at the men who think they run the Revolution.'

A shout of laughter erupted from a group of men behind her. 'We still do, you stupid *chipie*. Women have no rights.'

She rounded on her tormentors, and I took the opportunity to extricate myself from my bench partners and leave. Any further confrontation could easily have led to exposure. And now I had that added worry. I was saddened by Maxine's descent into the gutter, but I could do nothing to help her.

That was not the end of it. Only two days later I was urgently summoned by her, or rather, by a fellow *poissarde*, after a quarrel erupted in the fish markets. I almost refused to go. Maxine clearly resented me, for whatever inexplicable reason she'd dreamed up in a haze of brandy fumes. I had no wish to confront her now that she had so little control over her emotions. She was dangerous to herself, to others and, most particularly, to me.

Yet, she needed me. One of the not uncommon knife fights between the women gutting the fish had ended in serious injury to Maxine. By the description given me, there'd been severe blood loss and damage to her right arm.

Really, I had no choice. I picked up my bag and followed the messenger.

It was 31 March, a date that would forever live in my memory and be a reminder of great loss to my dear Armand.

The fish markets stank in the midday heat, and so did the meat market and the vegetable stalls. What little produce had come in from the fields and ponds was already rotting beneath the sun-soaked roofs. Long gone were the days of cheerful pandemonium when lines of drays filled the streets while waiting to be unloaded, and sellers fought for space for their wares, and buyers had their pick of the best that France could offer.

Now the *poissardes* fought for a place at the long tables impregnated with years of fish blood and refuse. Oil had polished the wood to glass, and scales and bones slid down easily into the great water tank placed to receive them further into the building. But there were fewer crates, and some of those not half-filled, and not enough work was available. That was the cause of the fights, that and the ugly temperament that seemed to be part of the *poissarde* culture.

Maxine lay in a pool of blood with her head on a jacket, surrounded by an unusually quiet crowd of women. With their stained and kilted skirts, bare arms and legs and smelling of their trade, they were a rabble, but a subdued one. Matters had become serious. I knelt down to examine my patient.

Dark eyes stared up at me, filled with pain and fear.

'What happened?' I asked, partly to cover my dismay as the blood continued to well through my exploring fingers.

One of the women answered grudgingly. 'She attacked me with her knife. She's crazy.'

'You accused her of taking your sausage,' said another.

'So she did. She's a food thief.' The accuser swung around. 'You all know it. She's been stealing from us every day. She should be denounced.'

'Who should be denounced?' a male voice asked.

I looked up to see two guardsmen pushing through the crowd to stare down at me and my patient.

The accusing woman pointed at Maxine. 'She's the one. She's a food thief, and she tried to kill me.'

Already pale from shock, Maxine's face turned a ghastly white. 'You lie, *salope!*' She raised her good arm and pointed at me. 'This is the one you want. This is the traitorous woman who disguises herself as a man to steal from the prisoners in her care.'

I was dumbstruck. My brain seemed to stop functioning as Maxine's malevolent gaze met mine. I knew that everyone would be focused on me, seeking my reaction.

One of the guards stepped forward and peered into my face. He said, 'I've seen you before, at the Conciergerie.'

'That's right,' Maxine said, pantingly eager. 'She's the doctor for the prisoners. But she's a woman and a thief.'

Slowly my brain began to function again as I said, 'This poor woman is very badly injured. She's not responsible for what she says.'

'I am … I am! Listen. Go to the Jew's tailoring shop in Saint-Martin and you'll find the jewels that she sold. I saw her go in there and come out with a full purse.'

It was my turn to blanch. Maxine knew about the jewels. But I could not explain how I came by them and so must be labelled a thief.

The guards moved forward, their hands on their swords. I could see they were impressed by Maxine's detail and were more than half decided to take me in.

I said, 'That may be so. Yet you must know how I spent that money: on the children, on the sick and needy people of the Saint-Antoine.'

'Another lie!' Maxine's voice had risen to a screech. 'If you want more proof that she's not to be trusted, tear open her shirt and see if she's not a woman taking up a man's rightful place.'

That was a change of attitude. I rose to my feet and automatically reached for my medical bag. My brain had picked up speed and now raced. I knew my position was perilous.

Maxine's denunciation had too much truth in it to be denied. There were only seconds between me and the bloody slope down to the guillotine.

My hand closed on the bulb of the spray bottle I'd filled only that morning with a tincture of valerian based in alcohol. As a weapon it lacked everything but one element – surprise. It would have to suffice.

I looked down at Maxine, at the self-satisfied expression of my betrayer, and my jaw dropped. *'Mordieu! Regardez.'*

The old tricks work best. As everyone obediently looked at her, I whipped out the spray, dropped the bag and sent the evil-smelling fluid jetting into the faces of the two guards. The mist of alcohol hit them. Staggering back with loud cries, they clawed at their eyes as the aroma of something like rotted cheese filled the air and fought with the local fish odour, creating a minor sensory hell. While the women gagged and the guards tottered, I took to my heels.

I knew I could outrun most of the heavier fishwives. However, the doorway by which I'd entered was blocked by the crowd of women, all armed with fish-gutting blades. I ran the opposite way.

I sped between the tables, bypassing the tank of entrails, my feet slipping on a film of fish scales. The heat wrapped around me like a stinking cloak, stealing my breath. Behind me rose shouts and the sound of pounding feet.

Les Halles was a huge complex of intersecting passageways between the various stalls, a geometric maze criss-crossed with alleys. I darted down one to my left, then zigzagged from side to side, working towards the nearest left-hand exit. I'd been here before and knew where it was. I also knew that if I lost myself in the various other markets under these roofs, as I easily could, I'd be completely disoriented. Swinging around one corner while steadying myself on a crate, I gashed my hand, but felt nothing. I leapt over piles of rubbish, landed in squashed cabbage leaves, slipped and regained my balance, and tore on without pause. The pursuit was gaining.

I heard a shot, and a piece of timber flew up only yards away. But there, just ahead of me, bright daylight gleamed. The doorway. I gave myself a moment to regain my breath, and to think ahead. I thought how I'd be silhouetted against that bright light, a fair target. With the instinct of a hunted fox, I turned in the opposite direction and ran further into the market.

Here I was in unknown territory. I could hear animals squealing and smell fresh blood, and ahead of me I saw the pale dead army of freshly hung carcasses, all in lines. Behind, came the sound of running footsteps. Without hesitation, I plunged into the ranks of dripping flesh and buried myself six rows deep, standing as still as any of the bodies hanging from the hooks.

Now I could take the time to be afraid. My heartbeat roared in my ears and sweat poured down my body. Fearing that I might topple over, I grasped a pair of fleshy pink trotters and held on tightly. The pervading smell of death reminded me that, if caught, I'd soon resemble one of those headless carcasses, soon be discarded as worthless in a trench filled with other nameless unfortunates.

Well, it wasn't going to happen to me! I clung to my naked pig and waited ... and waited. I heard the pack go past, howling, and still I waited. It was a full hour before I finally moved. I heard the sounds of closing down, of porters and butchers and vegetable sellers shouting *au'voir* to one another, or arranging to take a drink together. I mingled with the crowd leaving by a western door and, keeping to the gathering shadows, sped across the city towards the safety of Armand's rooms.

CHAPTER 21

I STROVE TO keep to a normal gait as I threaded my way through the backstreets towards Saint-Martin. I could do nothing about the pig blood staining my coat, and I kept to the shadows as much as possible. Fortunately, I went unnoticed by workers too intent upon either their supper or a visit to the nearest wine bar.

As I passed the dreaded Temple Prison I shuddered, fancying I could hear the groans of the inmates in their bleak, cramped cells. I thought how narrowly I'd escaped such incarceration, and wondered for how long I could remain free.

Although it seemed twice the distance, I eventually reached the tall, narrow house on the edge of the Saint-Martin section where Armand had his rooms. Although the street had seen better days, with dilapidated buildings crammed together like decayed teeth in a too-small mouth, the area was still far more salubrious than my own. I felt safe here. I dismissed the thought that Maxine might know this address, and my connection with it. If she did, my luck simply had run out.

I intended to alter my appearance by changing into a dress and shoes from the store of clothes I'd left here, and loosening my hair to my shoulders. I did not think the guards would be looking for a female. They'd last seen me running for my life in trousers, with coat-tails flying, and they would have that picture in their minds. No, the greater danger came from the denizens of the night. If anyone accosted me on the way home, I'd just have to trust once more to my fleetness of foot.

How I wished for Armand to be with me while I poured out my troubles, and to help me make plans. But he was engaged to dine with his friend, Danton, and would be late back. While flinging myself into my petticoats I composed a note for him, explaining that I must return to my lodgings to gather clothes and money and, most especially, my precious medical equipment and books, some of which had belonged to my father and were irreplaceable.

I knew the risk. I planned to reconnoitre carefully and to send in one of my street children to make sure no guards awaited me in Mère Poisson's kitchen. However, none of the fishwives had been my patient or knew where I lived.

I also had good reason to doubt Maxine's ability to give the guards my address. When I'd shouted 'Regardez!' I'd actually seen the veil of death creeping over her. The blood from her wound had continued to flow in an ever-widening pool, and my last view of her was of a pale face full of loathing, and a tide of crimson gushing from her mouth. She'd have been dead before the guards returned from their abortive search of the markets.

I put aside the thought of her dying with a lie on her lips and filled with hatred for a fellow being. I couldn't afford to think beyond my own safety.

Armand's comfortable, if shabby rooms were so inviting, I had to resist the temptation to curl up in his bed and forget the world and its dangers. Such a lovely bed, set high under a swathed canopy and down-filled to the point of voluptuousness. The rest of the furniture matched it in style and solidity. A bow-fronted bureau that held my clothes had been built by a master craftsman of the previous century, and the cracked frame of the mirror hanging above it was heavily gilded. Armand had even managed to acquire two watercolour landscapes that soothed the eye and were a reminder of the world we had once lived in.

Regretfully, I closed the door of the bedchamber behind me. Armand could not be put at risk. However, a grateful patient might take me in for a short time – just long enough for me to arrange an escape from Paris. I couldn't think beyond that. The stress of the horrible afternoon: the shock of betrayal, the race to escape, the interminable hour spent amongst fresh-killed carcasses, fearful that I'd be discovered at any moment, had told on me. I longed for Armand, but I could not wait for him. I'd send him a message later, when I had found a hiding place.

I cautiously opened the front door a crack and saw an empty street. Slipping out, I set off for the Rue Bitone.

Mère Poisson wept as I hurriedly stuffed clothing and books into a bag and looked around my Spartan chamber to see what must be left behind. I'd already organized my medical equipment in another bag. Even with few material things in my life, it seemed I must leave most of my meagre possessions for someone else. Perhaps Mère Poisson could find a use for a brocade waistcoat, a pewter tankard, a pair of Sèvres book ends. I considered a heavy *Works of Voltaire*, and reluctantly put it aside. I had no pack horse.

'Where will you go, *petite*? Must I lose everyone dear to me?' Mère Poisson sniffed and tried to stem the tears with her apron. Over past weeks, her kind face had lost its florid colouring. Now she seemed like a papier mâché puppet, worn out and abandoned to the weather.

I was sad to be leaving her, with her health slowly wasting away, and with no one to care about her. There were no adequate words to comfort this woman who had taken me in and treated me like her own child. Giving her a quick hug, I said, 'When I have found a place I'll let you know. Still … you know that I must leave Paris?'

She nodded desolately.

I added, 'You will pass on the message to Armand, as soon as he comes?' Of course she would. I'd already asked her twice. With nerves on edge, I simply had to repeat myself. I felt the sands in the hourglass running, running, and I wanted to run, too.

With bags ready at my feet, I had my purse in my hand, feeling its thinness, when someone banged loudly at the front door.

I froze. Not already! Surely there'd been no time….

A voice called, 'Doctor, you're needed. Open the door, Doctor.'

My shoulders sagged with relief, and I called back in a voice that shook, 'I'm coming.'

Rushing downstairs, I could not help but damn the inopportune caller. There was no time. I had to leave, now, before the inevitable visit from the guards. However, the sight of a man with a child in his arms, a broken-looking child with lolling head and limbs, sent all other thoughts flying. Beckoning the man in, I went ahead to the kitchen and swept the table clear.

'Lay the boy down and tell me what ails him.'

The burly fellow I recognized as a local carter gently deposited his burden on the table and stood back. Too distressed to comment, or even to note my petticoats, he hovered, literally wringing his work-worn hands. While the stumbling tale of disaster poured from his mouth, I stripped the lad and began examining the nasty wound in his chest. It seemed he'd been climbing up to a window – for reasons unspecified – but slipped and fallen on to a spiked railing. Luckily for him, only one spike had caught him, but it had gone deep. I just prayed that it had missed his lung.

Mère Poisson hurried in, puffing with the exertion of hastening downstairs. 'What is it? You must leave ... oh! *Le pauvre!* What happened to him?'

As the father once again explained, I inspected and cleansed the wound and decided that, as no vital organ had been affected, I could bind it up. I worked quickly, conscious of every passing moment when the risk to me increased. Finally, I finished. The child awoke and cried, as much from shock as from pain, but cheered up amazingly at the sight of a cup of chocolate.

With a few last instructions to the father, I raced up to my room for my baggage, clapped on my hat, and raced down again. A hurried kiss on Mère Poisson's cheek, and I sped out the back entrance, straight into the arms of the National Guard.

CHAPTER 22

WHY DIDN'T HE come? Curled up on the filthy straw of my cell, I marshalled every bit of my mental strength as a barrier to fear, willing Armand to feel my need for him.

I had been consigned to one of the Conciergerie's oubliettes, a dark, vermin-infested hole, a true dungeon. My questing fingers had felt the permanent dampness of seepage down the walls and the accretion of spongy growths. A rusted grate in the floor drained the water, and another grate in the door allowed me to imagine just the faintest suggestion of light from the passage beyond. The very air smelled of decay and despair.

But my surroundings hardly mattered. After hours of waiting, with hope fading, an emotional chill began to creep over me, sapping both will and energy. A myriad fears that had been stalking and circling in the background crept in to torment me. I pictured them as a pack of hyenas, snarling and jibing, telling me that no one could help, that I'd been abandoned, that soon I would take my last walk through the cruelly named *salle de la toilette* and out to the waiting tumbrel. And afterwards – death.

It was delayed shock, I suppose. More hours passed, and the debilitating numbness began to wear off. I kicked away the hyenas as my fighting spirit returned. I wasn't dead yet. I had *not* been abandoned. Once Armand discovered my plight, he would find a way to rescue me. Most likely, he'd have Danton speak for me. Yes, of course. A friend in high places, Armand had said, all those months ago, and he was right. Danton owed me a debt, and he was an honourable man. He'd have me released.

For a time I felt comforted, despite the darkness and the scrabbling sounds forcing me to crouch in the corner with knees drawn up and skirt tucked tight around my ankles. Anger, too, sustained me. The thieving guards had emptied my pockets, and without money I could not buy my way into a better cell. Still, Armand would have money.

Armand. All my hopes, large and small, were centred on him. I knew he would come.

It took him a whole day – the very longest day that I'd ever known. A dozen times I sprang up, hearing approaching foot-steps; they always died away, leaving me disappointed. However, many hours later I saw the flicker of lantern light on the wall as my cell door opened and Armand stepped in. The door crashed shut behind him, he dropped the lantern, and I flung myself into his arms, clinging as to a lifeline in a drowning pool.

'My poor darling. My Juliette.' He held me tightly, repeating my name over and over again. I felt the tremor running through his body as we sought comfort in each other's arms.

With my head buried in his neck I whispered, 'I feared that you would not come. I left a message at your rooms.' That was as close as I'd go to chiding him, but those empty hours of waiting had been so long.

His grip tightened. 'I did not return to my rooms. I did not know.' He drew me down with him on to the dirty palliasse. 'Mère Poisson's messenger eventually found me and I came at once. What brought this about?'

I kept my voice even. ''Tis a long story but, in brief, Maxine betrayed me. She denounced me before National Guardsmen and I had to run.'

Armand's mouth tightened. 'I knew she was not to be trusted. Tell me the full tale, my dear.'

I did so while he continued to hold me. I felt his rage as I told of the chase through the market halls and the hour I'd spent in terror amongst the animal carcasses. As I relived the agonizing fear of that pursuit, I heard him mutter a fearful oath. Yet, by the time I'd finished, I found I could detach from the memory and put it aside.

'Armand, what can we do? Can you think of any way to have me released?'

He shook his head. 'I've scarce had time to consider it.' He sounded wretched.

'What of Danton? He will surely stand as my friend. Can you not go to him—?' His expression stopped me. 'What is it, Armand?'

'So much has happened. I must tell you—' He paused.

'Tell me?' I prompted, distressed to see the glaze of tears in his eyes.

'George has had warning. Tomorrow he will be arrested and arraigned before the Convention.'

I felt the words like blows. Danton taken! The mighty lion of the Revolution pulled down, just as Armand had feared. And the consequences for me were dire. I'd pinned my hope of life on Danton's support.

Striving to overcome my shocking disappointment, I said, 'I'm so sorry. He is your friend and, I think, a good man at heart. Is there any hope? Will no one speak for him?'

Armand laughed harshly. 'He will speak for himself. Or rather, he'll roar through the Chamber of Deputies until those *miserables* who once cheered him shake in their boots. Of course, he cannot count upon their support. The cowards are too afraid for themselves. Robespierre has won, and Danton will die.' He put his hand to my cheek and stroked it. 'But you are the one who matters. You must be saved.'

I had no words. With Danton gone, we had lost our best leverage with the Revolutionary Tribunal. And it was they who decided who lived and who died. I could not help shuddering.

'Juliette! You must not despair.' Armand buried his face in my hair and said in a muffled tone, 'You know I would take your place in an instant. Dear God! There must be a way!'

Footsteps approached and the door swung back to reveal a jailer, a surly old man sporting evidence of his supper down the front of his coat and an attitude of no nonsense.

'You've had your time,' he said, picking up the lantern.

Armand rose, bringing me with him. 'Not so fast. What is the price of a decent cell with bedding and food sent in?'

The fellow's glowering expression lightened. 'That's something to be discussed, *citoyen*. Come with me.'

He ushered Armand out, banging the door on his protests that I should be immediately transferred. Over his shoulder Armand called as he was led away, 'I shall return very soon. Take heart, my love. There will be a way to free you.'

He'd gone, and I was left alone in the darkness to fend off the rats and the hyenas, and the horrible premonition that, despite whatever stupendous efforts Armand made, I soon would be just a statistic in the Committee's meticulous book of records.

The next morning the guard moved me to a ground-floor cell overlooking the women's courtyard, complete with sleeping cot. As per Armand's orders, hot food was brought to me, along with a few necessities, such as soap and linen.

For these I was grateful, but not comforted; my fear lay too heavily on me. However, I tried to hide it, filling the hours with visits to my fellow prisoners, and doing what I could for them without my medical equipment.

I was curious to see their reaction to my sudden apparent change of sex. For the most part, having expressed initial astonishment, they were amused and admiring. Only a few showed disgust, sweeping their skirts from my contaminating presence. As news of my masquerade spread, I had to repeat my story many times, and an interesting discussion began to flow on the rights of women versus conditioned, and often strictly enforced, behaviour.

With escape so much on my mind, I led the conversation to this, and was surprised to learn that there had been several attempts made, although not from the Conciergerie. Friends of important prisoners had organized raids on the Luxembourg and on two or three other prisons, with small success, it was admitted.

One of the women snorted at that, saying, 'If any did escape, no one ever knew it. The authorities simply denied it ever happened; and none of the other prisoners lived to tell the tale.'

I thought back to those horrific September riots, when the mob had overrun the prisons and clearly demonstrated that it was possible for such breaches to be made. There had even been a few escapees on that occasion, such as the priest who brought me news of Philippe, my poor brother. However, the cost had been too great. No one could wish to see another such murderous spree take place.

It hardly needed saying that, due to my total lack of importance, and to the strength of the Conciergerie's medieval walls, I soon dismissed any thought of an organized prison break on my behalf. It had been but a passing notion, born of a mind twisting and turning in search of a solution.

When Armand arrived late in the day, I whisked him into my cell, eager to hear his news. His smile did not deceive me. His haggard eyes and the rigid muscles in his cheeks revealed the stress he tried to cover. I led him to the cot and sat down beside him.

With his arm around my shoulders, he said, 'My dear, how do you fare? Are you receiving better treatment?'

'Thanks to you, I am. But tell me Danton's fate.' I held my breath, hoping that somehow the great man had confounded his enemies, yet knowing how little likelihood there was of such an outcome.

Armand said bitterly, 'The trial is a farce. He's being given no chance to defend himself. The result cannot be in doubt.'

'Then 'tis the end.'

'The end for him, and for France.' He turned and kissed me fiercely. 'Forget Danton. He is beyond help. But you … there will be a way to save you.'

The fear stirred in me. 'How? No one who goes before the Tribunal escapes.'

'I have given it much thought. *Mon Dieu*, I think of little else. 'Tis clear that only a corpse, or an apparent corpse leaves the Conciergerie without a ride in one of Samson's tumbrels.'

The mention of the country's chief executioner reminded me only too well of the occasions when I'd watched him work. I hurriedly blocked those memories, saying, 'You have not been trained to induce a trance state, Armand, and I can hardly mesmerize myself.'

'I was not proposing any such thing.' He looked at me searchingly. 'You are an unusual doctor, Juliette. Under your father's tutelage you learned many things not commonly known to the medical profession, and since then you have experimented widely in the field.'

I thought I knew what he was about to say. 'You want to know whether I have any more useful weapons in my medical armoury.'

He nodded. 'If you do, now is the time to use them. Because there is very little time left.'

I stiffened. 'What do you know, Armand? Is … is my name listed?'

The answer was in his expression.

'When?' I could scarcely form the word.

'You, along with about thirty bewildered peasant girls, will be tried and sentenced tomorrow.'

I stared unseeingly at him. Tomorrow! Execution always followed sentencing, immediately.

'Juliette! Listen to me.'

I realized that he was shaking me, and made myself focus again. 'Yes, I heard you.'

I moistened suddenly dry lips and said, 'There might be a way … a way so dangerous that I can only contemplate using it in dire emergency.'

'I believe this is sufficiently dire.' His grim face decided me. After all, one could only die once, and almost anything was preferable to public execution.

'Very well.' I had to make myself go on. The very contemplation of such a perilous procedure was enough to dry the throat. But I did continue, for some time, outlining my plan. I then had to deal with Armand's total rejection of the idea.

'No! I will not let you. 'Tis a monstrous risk.' He stood and paced the small area of the cell in agitation, ending before me. 'You cannot do it.'

'I can. I must. There is no other way.' I took his hands and drew him down beside me again. 'Armand, I will not be paraded through the streets, jeered at and spat upon, to climb those bloody steps to an ignoble death as amusement for the mob. I will gladly take the risk involved in my plan, if you will help me.'

I'd never before heard him groan. The sound seemed drawn from somewhere deep within, and it expressed, as nothing else could, the depths of despair that had engulfed him. I drew his head to my shoulder and found myself rocking him, like a child. Poor Armand, forced to flee the country he loved, his deep-rooted beliefs slaughtered, the woman he loved in danger of suffering a terrible end.

But Armand was too strong to be beaten by fate. Within moments he had detached himself, shaking his head, as if to clear it, and saying, 'Forgive me. Of course there is no choice. You are going to live, my dear, and together we'll make a new life in another country. Some day we may return to help rebuild France into her pride.'

'Yes, my love. Some day.' Prophecy or prayer? Who knew? Only the Angel of Mercy, if he happened to be looking. Because it would take heavenly intervention if I were to survive tonight's perilous enterprise.

CHAPTER 23

ARMAND'S HAND TREMBLED as he picked up the poisoned barb. He let it drop back into its groove and wiped the sweat from his forehead. The skin across his cheekbones appeared stretched to tearing point, like a chicken skin tightened over a drum, and his eyes burned hotly. He seemed to be at a loss, saying, 'I've never before hesitated. This is the hardest thing I have ever done.' He looked down at me. 'My dear, I must first make a slit in your skin so that I may plunge the barb deep into the muscle. That way the poison will enter the bloodstream more quickly.'

'Then do it … now, while my courage holds.'

He grasped his knife and bent over me, pulling aside my gown. I felt the sting as the blade sliced into my shoulder muscle. I gasped as the barb was thrust deep.

'How long?' His voice already seemed to come from afar.

'Soon.' I could feel the poison trickling through me, insidious as an incoming tide creeping ever further up the shore. My heart laboured with the terror I could not suppress.

I had not told Armand my worst fear. Death would mean oblivion. I'd faced the idea and come as close as I could to terms with it. Yet there was a fate that, for me, held the ultimate in horror – paralysis. Accurate timing was so important, and I knew so little about the action of this poison. What would it mean to survive, only to find that I'd lost the use of, say, a limb? How would the loss of such mobility affect my work? Would Armand feel differently towards me? What if all my extremities were affected? A monstrous thought that I thrust from me.

As Armand withdrew the barb, I began counting slowly to sixty, twice. Then, ''Tis happening, Armand! My fingers and toes grow numb. Call for the bearers. Call now!'

Moments later I'd lost control of my facial muscles. From the corner of my unblinking eyes I saw him rush to the door, shouting for the body bearers.

Returning quickly, he strapped me down to the board from my cot and twitched my hood across my eyes, just as the men arrived. They raised the board and I left my cell for what I hoped was the last time.

The journey across the courtyard seemed endless. Twice we were stopped as women I'd befriended and helped demanded an explanation of my sudden demise. Their shocked voices expressed true regret and, in one or two cases, genuine grief. I could only beg them silently to let us go. In my head I was counting off the seconds. Fifteen minutes only before Armand must apply the antidote. Almost four of those minutes had passed already.

What if the sailor who sold me the *karare* had been wrong? What if this poison should work more swiftly on me? No! That way lay madness. I had to trust to what I'd been told and keep counting.

Finally I heard the gates unlocked, then locked again behind us. Through the hood, I was conscious of the dimness as we entered the prisoners' hall. All the while I grew colder and more numb. Now my limbs had turned to useless appendages. I felt suffocated beneath the hood, although I knew the poison could not yet have reached my lungs.

Another two minutes gone. And the most appalling thought

burned an acid path across my mind. What if I suffered *total* paralysis? *Mère de Dieu*! I might survive as no more than a mind locked in a useless body – never to be wife, mother, life companion. The woman that Armand loved, articulate, independent, professionally competent, would no longer exist. How could he possibly deal with such a cruel burden? And how could I bear to watch the slow death of our love in his eyes? Dear God! Let it not happen.

While struggling to overcome these bitter thoughts, I noticed a change. It seemed that, with the loss of sensation, my other senses had become more alive, and the sounds around me clearer. The shuffling footsteps of the bearers and their heavy breathing overlaid voices of the guards, the harsh coughing of someone in the throes of *la grippe*, and further off, a young voice singing – a prisoner, perhaps? The melody was half familiar.

My heart lurched. Suddenly I was transported back to an evening far in the past. I sat warmly wrapped upon my mother's knee at the fireside while she dried my hair and sang about a bird in its nest in an apple tree. I knew that sweet voice, even though I'd not heard it for almost two decades.

Tears welled in my dried out eyes. 'Oh, *Maman*,' I whispered, or thought I did.

The bearers halted. We'd arrived at the checking area. My hood was flung back and I stared into the fat, unshaven face of a National Guardsman. Behind him, the clerk was taking my details, given by Armand in a calm tone which surely belied his inner urge to hasten from this place.

I waited for the guard's thumb in my eye socket, knowing it would hurt, but there'd be no response.

His shout made me jump inwardly. '*Hola!* This one lives. See the tears upon her cheeks?'

The desperation of that moment still haunts my dreams. It

had all been for nothing. We'd come so close, but now both Armand and I would die.

'Not so.' Armand's voice was easy, conversational. Only the dear Lord knows how he achieved it. ''Tis a purely automatic response to exterior stimulus of the ocular nerves by a change in temperature, quite common in a fresh corpse. If you carry out the usual test with your thumb, you will see that there is no reaction. Or, better. I shall demonstrate that there is no life in those eyes.' He beckoned to another guard. 'Bring me that torch, citoyen.'

Lining up the two men, he explained to the doubter, 'The hall is dim and you will see that in this man's eyes the pupils – the dark centres – are quite large. You agree?'

The first guard grunted, reluctantly.

I was beginning to panic. Still counting desperately, I saw light bloom on the groined roof above me as Armand picked up a lamp from the secretary's table. I knew he must not appear to hasten, but the minutes were racing by. Half our time gone already.

Armand said, 'Watch what happens when I shine this light in your comrade's face.'

The man moved out of my view. Still, I heard him exclaim, 'Vraiment! The black dot shrinks like a snail into its shell.'

'Exactly.' Lamp in hand, Armand bent over me, his face impassive, saying, 'Now I will do the same for this corpse.'

The guard thrust his face into mine. His expression clearly said that he wasn't going to be tricked by any fancy hocus-pocus.

I stared helplessly back at him as Armand brought the lantern within an inch of my nose.

'You see?' he said. 'The pupils have not moved. No one can control that reaction voluntarily. Life is extinct. Now may I dispose of this corpse and go home to my dinner?'

I was ringed by curious faces. For at least an aeon that was all of twenty seconds they watched and waited until, tired of the non-event, they gave up.

Finally, with an annoyed exclamation, the clerk picked up his pen. I heard it scratch on the paper. Relief flooded through me; and so did the poison. It seemed to have gathered speed, now spreading from limbs to torso and moving steadily towards my lungs. I fancied I felt its touch there, and suddenly I could not breathe! I was suffocating! That wretched sailor had misjudged the speed of the reaction. My life was unravelling, with but a thread left.

The bearers took one step forward. I realized that, after all, I was still taking shallow breaths, aligned with my counting. Three more minutes. There was yet time.

'Tenez!' The surly guard, my nemesis, still exhaled garlic vapour into my face, obviously unconvinced. I felt I could have counted the whiskers on his stubbled chin, the veins in his wine-bibber's nose. I wanted to scream.

The bearers halted. And it was then the great doors to the entrance hall were flung back like so much matchwood, and men flooded in, shouting: 'Danton! Give us Danton!'

At the sound of gunshots, I was unceremoniously dropped as the bearers fled. Footsteps raced by me; I saw the flare of fire as torches were thrown in the guards' faces; someone screamed, a long drawn-out wail of agony; booted feet stepped on my legs and a man, his throat gaping from an awful wound, fell across me. Armand threw him off and attacked the straps, freeing me from the board. He then dragged me with him across the stone floor to crouch behind the clerk's desk.

The clerk lay there, stunned, clutching his belly leaking blood and intestines. The clash of weapons, shots and screams, and the continuing call for Danton created uproar, drowning Armand's voice. It hardly mattered. I'd lost the count. We were trapped and there was no time left. My life thread had been cut.

Ever after I wondered whether, in that moment of terrible knowledge, Armand knew my despair. Certainly, he acted with frantic speed. Plucking the second barb from its container, he bared my shoulder and stabbed into the slit. Too late, I thought. I was experiencing my last few moments on this earth. At least I was in Armand's arms; and from a full heart I sent him all the love that I could not, and never would be able to express.

Sounds seemed to fade. The light was going. This must be how life ended. I wanted to look into Armand's face. I wanted it to be my last sight on earth. But he was nowhere. He'd gone.

Desolate, I suddenly realized that I could feel movement! My body was alive! I was being carried out of the chaos of the prison hall.

The chill night air was a benediction as it flowed into my lungs. I drank it in like nectar … blessed, life-giving air. The first pale stars of evening appeared above my head. I heard Armand's panting breath as he ran with me away from that terrible prison, that gateway to death. I was free. At that moment, nothing else mattered, not my still-leaden body, my useless limbs, the deadened muscles of cheeks and eyes. I could breathe. I would live.

Seated in the waiting carriage, Clara greeted my appearance with a glad cry, and Mère Poisson reached out to help settle me comfortably along one seat. I could now feel my lower extremities, and my eyes were behaving normally. I could smile at Clara, although my voice was not yet in working order. Inwardly, I shouted aloud with joy. The antidote had worked. I was almost whole again.

Armand wasted no time. Having assisted Mère Poisson to alight, and kissed her cheek in farewell, as I would like to have done, he sprang up on the box, saying, 'We're not yet beyond their reach. That ill-advised attempt to storm the prison and free George will inevitably fail. The fools! Too disorganized to realize that he'll be returned to the Luxembourg until he's sentenced. Soon the guards will be chasing them through the streets. We must stay ahead and reach the gates before they close, or we'll be trapped.'

He whipped up the horses and headed south for the Porte Royale. Night was almost upon us. Would we make the gates before they were shut? So close, and yet we could still lose the last round in this deadly game.

I remember little of our race for life. I'd been through so much, suffered the crazy, dizzying cycle of desperate fear and raised hopes suddenly dashed. For the moment, I clung to the thought of freedom from all that insecurity and closed my mind to the alternative.

Clara, white-faced and too aware for a child so young, hung on to me as the carriage bounded over the cobbles, taking the corners at a wicked speed. I could feel her fear and tried to comfort her, whispering that we'd soon be safe, that we could trust Armand to care for us. I don't know whether she heard. I fancied that her arms tightened around my neck.

By then I was dealing with another blow. While most of me had recovered, my right arm remained paralysed.

Pinching and thumping, I willed it to come to life. Clara watched me, wide-eyed, sensing my piercing disappointment. The cruelty of it, at the last minute, after I thought I'd won free. 'Twas bitterly unfair. To have risked everything, overcome so much and be left a partial cripple. It was hard.

I told myself that I had my life. I still could work, even if hampered by my useless limb. I called upon all my strength of will, my gratitude for my life, my love and the chance to begin again. I was a survivor, wasn't I? Survivors did not cavil at a check, they overcame it.

I'd reached this stage in my thinking when the horses slowed to a more decorous pace. We were approaching the Porte Royale, and our final point of danger that night.

Were the gates still open?

The demand came for us to halt, and: 'You're too late. Gates are closing for the night.' There was satisfaction in the guard's tone.

Armand proffered papers, spoke placatingly. Perhaps money changed hands. The carriage door was flung open and a guardsman's head appeared in silhouette against the sunset sky. Clara shrank back as he pulled roughly at my coverlet and stared at me, saying, 'Your man says you're sick. What's wrong with you? Why do you leave Paris so late?'

Armand's voice floated down from the box seat of the carriage. 'I told you, *citoyen*. I'm taking my cousin to her family at Ramolles to be nursed. She's sick of a fever, but I fear 'tis something worse.'

I managed a hoarse cough and, with my left hand surreptitiously squeezed the wound in my shoulder, making it ooze. Letting my gown slip aside I displayed the result. In the poor light it might have been anything.

'See here, *citoyen*,' I croaked. 'Does it seem to you a buboe? Tell me 'tis not so.' I raised my voice piteously. 'Tell me I'm not going home to die.'

The guard's head withdrew with the speed of a rabbit spotting a snake at its burrow. 'Plague!' he shouted. 'Get this pestilent carriage out of the gates. Now!'

The horses moved forward with a jerk and the carriage rolled through the closing gates, leaving the city I'd entered with such high hopes, and speeding on out into the darkening countryside.

The first ship, Armand had said. It turned out to be something less grand, a fishing boat out of Le Havre, smelly, slippery and open to a spray-laden wind. It did not matter. Nothing mattered as, safe in the circle of Armand's arms, with Clara in my lap, I turned my face towards a foreign shore. We'd won free. We were together, unharmed and with the courage to face our uncertain future.

What is more, that morning the fingers of my right hand had twitched. By nightfall they were able to clasp Armand's hand at my waist.

'Well, my dearest of loves,' he said in my ear. 'This is the start of a new life. Do you have plans already?'

'Certainly. I believe we should go into practice together, blending our individual skills. There are certain new methods I've not yet tried; and I believe that England has plants with the most amazing medicinal properties. Clara must go to school, of course. Yet if she should show any tendencies towards a medical career, we should foster them.'

He gave a mock groan. 'I'm to wed a rabid feminist, and already I'm outnumbered.' He smiled down at the child, asleep on my knee, then added more sternly, 'But no more experimentation upon yourself, ever. I could never go through that again.'

I thought of those interminable minutes when I'd lingered between life and death and Armand had fought for me, and I shuddered. 'Never again. You have my promise. I have too much to lose.'

As the coast of England rose up on the horizon, I turned my face to his and sealed that promise with a heartfelt kiss.